Andrew Hewett Malcolm Lomas was born in Doncaster in 1976. He studied Sociology at the University of Leicester and has been a successful teacher of Sociology since 2002. For a number of years, he was a successful athlete, but now enjoys walking, swimming and foreign travel. After spending over a decade in Manchester, he has now settled in Salisbury. *The Near Future* is Andrew's first novel.

For Mum and Dad

Andrew Hewett Malcolm Lomas

THE NEAR FUTURE

AUSTIN MACAULEY PUBLISHERS™

LONDON · CAMBRIDGE · NEW YORK · SHARJAH

A CIP catalogue record for this title is available from the British Library.

ISBN 9781528908917 (Paperback)
ISBN 9781528908924 (Hardback)
ISBN 9781528959087 (ePub e-book)

www.austinmacauley.com

First Published (2020)
Austin Macauley Publishers Ltd
25 Canada Square
Canary Wharf
London
E14 5LQ

Part One

Chapter 1

Here you are again staring at your whiskey-struck eyes with knowing distain. They're a little yellow, not so you'd know once you've showered and got those neatly pressed clothes on, which you half remember preparing last night. You even manage a grin after applying some aftershave over two days' worth of stubble. Obviously, this hangover won't last long, and you know any inevitable dark mood will pass before you arrive. The start early, finish early rule you adhere to, usually works.

When you are ushered in at 8.30am he's sat behind his desk, in his crisp navy suit, eyes down, roaming through paper with his distinctive red pen.

"Take a seat, Sergeant," he instructs; the eyes still down.

"I hear you are currently observing one of the Government's more colourful characters?" he continues.

"Yes Sir, three weeks now," you reply noticing that the grey eyes are now up, keenly observing you directly. You have only been assigned to the department for a handful of months, but the look is familiar and you know how to respond.

"He's very predictable at present sir. Just seems to be the drink and drugs at the moment. No signs of women, or men for that matter. The Administrator for Environmental Reproduction appears to have an addiction to high-level stimulants and is consuming up two bottles of 75% proof alcohol a day. Clearly if this continues, the Administrator's ability to serve His Majesty's reformed Government becomes hindered." A fairly standard response you feel, as the office humidity causes a cold sweat to pour down your forehead.

"Well, that's all very interesting, but I feel your abundant talents may be better served elsewhere. You will report to Immigration at 9.15." You feign a perplexed frown, which has no impact.

"Well?" he enquires.

That's all it takes and you don't question these ambiguous orders because there isn't any point. It doesn't take much to fall. The destitute are there to be seen on the crammed trams you ride on daily, and you're clever enough to know how unfair it is, but smart enough to realise not to think on it too much.

It's a ten-minute wait before you're ushered into the Minister for Immigration and Environment's Office, by a slim awkward young man. Once in the room you immediately notice there are three people situated next to each other in an arch, like they're preparing for an interview post they've already decided on.

On the left you notice a serious looking middle-aged man with a neatly trimmed beard. The man to the right you deduce to be a government recorder, in front of him is a wafer thin laptop, documenting your short walk to an adjacent seat, obviously intended for you.

Your attention is drawn towards the man in the centre, who is wearing what you immediately recognise as an expensive lightweight suit, neatly made to measure round his stocky frame. The multi coloured linen tie signifies to you that this man is under the media microscope, and a sickly smile confirm that this is the Department Minister. He makes a warm hand gesture for you to take a seat.

"Please take a seat, sorry for the delay, we've had numerous reports from Iceland indicating that sea levels will significantly rise over the next month. Well Sergeant, as you can imagine."

After taking your seat, you cast your eye round the room, noticing the unnecessary size of the place. Behind all the obligatory government propaganda is a large Chesterfield sofa needlessly pushed towards the back wall, next to a cabinet containing an assortment of different alcohols.

You are offered a drink of whiskey, which despite the hour you accept, and having taken a small sip of the most expensive blend you've tasted in years, you allow the Minister's Secretary, sitting on the left to begin.

"You are here because we believe you can neutralise a rather tricky situation for our Minister. It won't strike you as news that the country is undergoing drastic but necessary changes; we can no longer ignore the obvious political and social problems that have come about since what we'll call environmental developments. The public and more importantly the media can't be oblivious when whole communities and towns are decimated."

"What do you want?" You reply curtly. The bearded man looks slightly annoyed, but before he can issue a response, the Minister puts his hand onto his aid's arm, ushering his silence and then takes over.

"What I want as a Minister and want my Government desires, is for you to observe a rather troublesome group of individuals. There has been, for a number of months a disgruntled group of militants disrupting the relative peace of our city. Government offices ransacked, trams derailed, government marketing defaced."

"Where do I come into this?" You enquire somewhat more politely than your previous question.

"The explosion of the newly built capsule flats in the worker's sector has meant this problem can't be ignored by us or the media anymore. We would like you to find, observe and eliminate this problem before it gets out of hand."

The Minister having noticed, he has your full attention, stops and then watches the filer place a closed document in your lap, which you open to see the picture of a face you recognise. You reach for your whiskey and drink the remaining contents, before looking up at the Minister.

"So we can assume that you are familiar with the subject of this enquiry?" The Minister asks, following a long pause. After nodding, you stare back coldly at all three men, waiting for the next question.

"The subject's name, as you're obviously aware is William Dudek, a third generation immigrant Pole. He is responsible or at least suspected of the recent destruction of four capsule apartments, violent civil unrest incidents and numerous digital acts of fraud, which can't be calculated."

"We estimate in the region of two million Euros," interrupts the bearded man who has a distinctly intense look on his face. The Minister continues, "You are in an excellent position to find this man and his associates, and then obliterate this problem. Sergeant, our society is in a constant flux, we live on a balance between stability and chaos. This kind of behaviour will not be tolerated."

"Why not get the police to deal with this? I'm a government official. This is not my jurisdiction." You say in a jaded attempt to be diplomatic. The bearded man now leaps from his chair, like an attack dog.

"You're not in a position to debate; you are also fortunate not to be in prison. The past can sometimes catch up with you Sergeant, very quickly. The unique talents, which you possess and old friendship with this man will be utilised to neutralise this situation, unless of course you wish to relinquish your duties," he barks, whilst his face reddens. The Minister feigns a sympathetic look at you, and you nod back acknowledging your predicament. An aggressive response would be gratifying but not self-serving. They are obviously fully prepared to any negative response with a further counter threat. In light of this you remain silent and listen.

The Minister turns and looks awkwardly at his two assistants.

"I'd like a quiet word alone with the Sergeant, gentlemen please," he sternly commands.

The recorder speedily closes his laptop and assembles his equipment, leaving the room hurriedly. The bearded man makes a more grandiose display of being disgruntled, but departs the room no less subserviently.

In a slow deliberate manner the Minister takes your glass and pours you both another large measure of whiskey. He then slides his chair closer to where you sit, undoing the top button of his pale blue linen shirt.

"I must apologise for Mr Poe's behaviour, he's an efficient but slightly blunt man." You nod, knowing he wishes to continue.

"I wouldn't want you to think we are threatening you into this assignment Sergeant. Your intimate knowledge of the subject simply makes you a suitable candidate. You do see don't you?" You nod a second time, and attempt to look back with empathy.

"Please understand you will have the full backing of the department in this matter. Any bureaucratic obstacles you encounter are dealt with." He hands you a document and points at his own signature at the bottom. The wry grin on your face is genuine and you slowly fold the paper, before placing it inside your pocket.

"Mr Poe will be observing your progress from a suitable distance. All daily reports can be mailed directly to him and the Office of Administration will issue you with a new gun. Well Sergeant, all that remains is for me to wish you good luck." You finish off your whiskey before shaking his hand firmly, and leave the room.

Chapter 2

It's the dark evening now, and you are staring out at the city from your balcony. Despite the late hour you can still see the coastline. Even from this distance you spot people setting up make shift tents on the pale sand. Several people have simply lay down on the beach and fallen asleep. You speculate that they are either drunks or just obstinate enough in their refusal to admit this will be their permanent residence.

This triggers a memory from your past. Beach football with friends, played every day after school on a beach that the government now warns citizens is a 'high risk' zone. The bleakness of the city landscape renders any such nostalgia obsolete and you return inside to your work desk.

On your desk is a whiskey, next to an assortment of documents. You raise the heavy based glass to your lips and take a large sip. It's taken you an afternoon in the Cleveland Arms and two liberal measures of whiskey to gather your senses after this morning's ambush. The photograph stares back at you, it says 'The Target' in bright red print and then a name three inches below, in stark bold capitals.

William Dudek had at first seemed to be a nondescript man. When you first met him he barely spoke. You were both being briefed on a planned attack of a government welfare unit ten years ago. It had been planned meticulously, with the intention of disrupting legislation that intended to further reduce the amount of second-generation immigrants claiming benefits. At the time it had been described to you as another step in what appeared a realistic revolution.

Everyone called him the 'kid' because of his youthful face, which was blemished by a three-inch scar on his left cheek. He was of medium build but had broad shoulders that contradicted the boyish looks. His hair was strikingly blonde and neatly cropped, military style.

It was during a mission that Dudek came to life. You remember his child like grin as he placed explosives under a desk on the fourth floor of the Immigration Office, in midnight darkness. His high-pitched laugh was infectious; as you had to keep relighting matches so you could make your way in the pitch black. When you both looked on in awe, from a safe distance as the fourth floor burst into flames he seemed to glow with pride. He believed so wholeheartedly that what you were all doing was just.

This was in conflict with your unique brand of apathy. You had both been raised in capsule flats, where privacy was a priceless luxury. The government's marketing campaign had tried to spin the capsules, as examples of 'social cohesion' There were the token gesture success stories, young boys and girls from the capsules who'd gone on to play football for their country or been a war hero. Some capsules had even been named after a former resident, but anyone living in one knew them as cramped humid beehives.

The kid was easy to become friends with. He had a breezy charisma, and once he realised you were both competent and willing to share a glass of whatever was to hand, you'd earned his respect. Soon enough, despite the age gap you became inseparable and insisted that you work together on all assignments. You were at least fifteen years his senior, the specifics never came up in conversation.

Dudek believed that things could be improved. He was honestly outraged at the legitimation of poverty, seething with anger at government bureaucrats who blindly ignored the starving misfortunates that begged on the trams every morning. The inevitable causalities were collateral damage. As the news announced the deaths of three government officials killed in an explosion, you looked to the kid for a reaction. The attack had been planned on the Department of Environmental Damage that had recently increased poll tax in all inner city capsules months in advance. The explosion was scheduled for dawn. Unfortunately, an incompetent drunk carried out the assignment and the entire ground floor erupted, killing three men just after eight.

The kid showed no signs of sympathy as the news focused on the backgrounds of the officials. He argued that if the attacks made the government re-evaluate the poll tax decision then the mission was successful. This was not how you saw it; you had a young son who lived in the British Southern Islands. These men had families too, friends whom they would see at weekends. They would have planned their future. It was the system that was at fault and bundling attacks like this wouldn't get sympathy for the cause.

Dudek had a violent streak; you remember how he'd beaten a man savagely to the floor. They'd asked you both to give a gentle reminder to a former agent that the work he'd done would remain confidential. There was fear the man would become boastful and loose lipped after too much bourbon.

The kid had seen this as a chance to settle an old score. The man had been fond of teasing the kid, nothing too hostile. Simply the kind of banter middle-aged men believe younger men should go through, a rite of passage. This isn't how the kid saw it. The moment the door opened you would begin your passive aggressive approach, finishing off with a calm but direct verbal threat.

The door opened and Dudek sucker punched the man on the nose. He then began hitting fiercely towards the kidneys. The bewildered man let out high-pitched gasp before collapsing to his knees.

"Hold on kid, what's this about?" He whispered as blood poured from his nose. The kid bent down slowly to him and whispered something in his ear before kicking his stomach. The whole time the kid's face remained placid and cold.

It was only two days later that William Dudek was advised by the leaders to leave the city. The incident had received no media coverage but the man's wife had reported the incident. The kid accepted this decision and spent the next year in the rural sector completing menial administration work for the cause.

The last time you talked was over whiskey hours before he left. He spoke on how frustrated he'd become and how the organisation could be more proactive, you remember nodding reassuringly before shaking his hand. He grinned back at you then walked away with purpose.

In his absence you enjoyed each assignment less than the last. The enjoyment and adrenalin rushes you'd had working with the kid were gone, the drinking increased and you became jaded. In the end it was no surprise you were caught. The government had been watching you for months and presented you with a simple dilemma, prison or tell them as much as you knew about how the cause. The names of the leaders, individual weaknesses, conflicting ideologies and the movement's infrastructure and you gave them everything.

In return you have the rank of sergeant and a government job as an observer. There were other material gains. A spacious apartment in a desirable location, a collection of 'made to measure' suits, leather soled shoes and a pension. The navy suit you intend to wear is already hung up over a light pink shirt and navy tie, and you gulp down your whiskey and decide on an early night.

Chapter 3

After drinking two cups of coffee and some squashed juice you pull up the navy tie close to your neck and leave the apartment. It's not yet ten o'clock but the morning air is already dry with heat. The working population have arrived at the various government departments so the tram seats are almost empty. The late morning commuters are a collection of the elderly and destitute. The tram glides further away from the city out to the coast and the driver eventually announces that you've arrived at the final destination on the line.

There is a young man covered in filth, laid on the floor next to the tram door. His reddened eyes fix on you and you gently toss him a Euro before exiting the tram. The splintered wooden platform is covered with a thin layer of sand. At the far end of the platform you notice a white haired man sweeping the sand back onto the beach. There are discarded alcohol bottles sporadically protruding from the distant sea. The beach is largely inhabited apart from a few families cooking fish on makeshift frying pans.

As the dry morning warmth turns to smouldering midday heat you put on shades and dab sweat beads from your head with an ice white handkerchief. The beach is about one mile long and you can see your destination clearly. It is one of five beach bars. The first is the largest and most exclusive, with an attractive couple sharing a bottle of wine perched up in an ice bucket. The two middle bars are more modest establishments with a handful of customers sat outside drinking coffee. The fourth bar seems to have recently closed down, but it is the smallest bar at the end that you head to.

Tropicana Bar has seen better days. The outdoor tables haven't been cleaned and the chair legs are rust-covered.

"Coffee?" asks the rake thin waiter as he removes rain soaked cigarettes from an ashtray.

"No. Thank you, but I am looking for George Saunders." The waiter's formal manner fades and he grins back and points to the man inside sat near a snooker table. When you walk into the dimly lit bar you recognise him sat face up, his eyes closed leaning back against a burgundy leather chair. There is a near empty bottle of whiskey on the table in front of him and a smashed glass on the floor besides him. He looks almost the same as you remember. There are a few more white hairs in the stubble that rest on the gaunt liver stained face, but it's definitely him.

The noise you make sliding a chair along the bar floor causes him to wake abruptly. The bleak eyes stare back with angry recognition.

"Hi, George. I thought I'd find you here amidst the seaside and scotch." He continues to glare menacingly but offers no response.

"Can I get a large glass of bourbon, please?" you shout back to the waiter.

"That's if there is any left?" you whisper at your inebriated solo audience.

"Hair of the dog?" George Saunders nods back.

"Make that two large bourbons, please."

The waiter brings over two generous measures of whiskey and places them on the nearest table.

"I'll take care of these George. I imagine you're between jobs at the moment," you say whilst handing the waiter a twenty-Euro note.

"What do you want, you bastard?" he gnarls at you. He gulps down his whiskey and stares waiting for your answer

"I'm looking for the kid." His menace evaporates into a large drunken grin and he bursts into laughter.

"I bet you are. That's why you've come looking for old George eh?" He clasps his hands together and laughs loudly; you drink your bourbon and gesture to the waiter for another round. He continues,

"I heard you were a government man now, running from one department to another. The desk job, yearlong tram pass, umbrella, government postcode and a tidy little pension, eh?" He laughs again.

"I'm looking for the kid," you repeat. George Saunders is in a terrible state. His black lightweight cotton trousers have small tares around the knees. The unwashed shirt is an ill-advised white that makes the alcohol stains more obvious. His face is ashen pale aside from liver stains around the nose and the whites of the eyes are devastated after years of abuse.

"They've sent you here in that fancy suit to old George, eh? Why don't you piss off?" He sways back into his chair and you grab him back up by the collar impatiently.

"Listen you rodent unless you tell me where he is I can personally guarantee that your daytime drinking sojourns will be over. How long do you think an old lush like you lasts in prison?" You punch him firmly in the stomach. He falls off his chair into the foetal position and vomits onto the bar floor. He groans moving from side to side, his arm holding the stomach and you stand above him and gently whisper in his ear.

"I don't want to hit you again, George." He pulls himself to his feet and slumps back into his chair as you hand him your handkerchief. He wipes his mouth dry then takes a sip of whiskey as you lean in to repeat yourself.

"I'm looking for the kid."

"Yeah. I saw him about two weeks ago," he says despondently and you raise an inquisitive eyebrow ushering him to continue.

"I saw him in that posh new cocktail bar up town. That big Irish fella from the old days owns it."

"Flannery?"

"Yeah. The kid was there throwing money around, buying everyone drinks," Saunders continued.

"Who was he with?" you ask.

"That crazy bastard with the eye patch and a slim bloke with red hair who used to hang with you sometimes."

The descriptions are apt and you recognise both men. The man with the eye patch is a fourth generation Pole Andrei Makowski, known to the few friends he has, as 'Mak' a sadist whom apparently lost his left eye in a drunken fight over a snooker game. The slim red haired man is an old friend Pete Baker, who you reckon to be in his late thirties now.

"Did you speak to them, George?"

"I spoke to the kid about the old days and the cause. He said they'd got soft and needed to hit the right targets."

"Did they speak about me?" you ask.

"The kid said he understood why you'd done it, but that didn't mean he liked it. The big bloke with the patch has no love for you."

Saunders smiled about this last part. He attempts to hand back your handkerchief but you decline and begin walking out. Before leaving, you hand the waiter another twenty-Euro note and instruct him to keep the drinks coming for George.

"I'd stay away from the kid you bastard. They'll kill you!" You grin ruefully and walk outside onto the sand.

The heat has intensified and the other bars have more customers sitting outside than before. There are still several families either cooking or making shelter for the evening. When walking past the more exclusive bar you see Mr Poe. He is sitting outside the bar under an umbrella sipping an espresso ushering you to join him and you take your place on the opposite side of the table. On the table is a wafer thin laptop. He's in a pale blue three-piece suit, white cotton oxford shirt and red woollen tie. He has a large panama hat tilted on his head and silver-rimmed sunglasses cover his eyes.

"Can I get you a drink, Sergeant?"

"A large black coffee, please."

Mr Poe makes eye contact with a strikingly attractive girl with short blonde hair. She takes his order and in short time brings you a coffee and Poe a second espresso. Mr Poe stirs his drink slowly and leans in.

"What are you doing down here, Sergeant? I do hope government money isn't being wasted on your bar tab." He removes his glasses and squints at you.

"I'm tracing Dudek's recent steps sir. I didn't know I was being followed," Poe nods his head disapprovingly and whispers through gritted teeth.

"Do you really think we are going to let a self-confessed crook like you run amok at our expense? The assignment demands results. It may not be apparent to a man like you Sergeant but this city is in decay. Every Euro spent must be accountable. Why were you in that bar, Sergeant?"

You can feel your temper rising and would like nothing more than to punch this obnoxious man to the floor. This would achieve nothing and you opt for diplomacy.

"I was interrogating someone sir. This person had recently made contact with Dudek. The suspect was called George Saunders. He worked on the peripheries of the cause but could never be trusted with important assignments." His mood changes and he begins recording this new information with fervour on his laptop. Poe then looks up.

"This assignment could really bolster your career. This would mean you wouldn't always be Sergeant. I can personally recommend the benefits of being Officer Class." He then gives a sickly smile that makes your stomach churn. Poe continues,

"Guaranteed Premier class seats on trains, air conditioned section on the trams. No one can afford to sit in the Premier class tram compartment; you practically have it to yourself."

"It sounds idyllic sir," you reply sarcastically. His veneer of politeness evaporates rapidly.

"What is your next move, Sergeant?" he asks.

"I intend to visit the owner of the bar these men have apparently been frequenting. Michael Flannery." He looks confused.

"Flannery wouldn't show up on official records sir. He has never been a member of the cause and keeps his hands very clean. He's a pragmatic man and will not be quite as hostile as my last lead."

"Good. I will not be observing your progress tonight but look forward to seeing a detailed report no later than midday tomorrow. Please include a list of any expenses," he states before efficiently folding his laptop.

He hands you a generous amount of money for the drinks and then leaves. He doesn't shake your hand and you're grateful for this. Then you stroll leisurely to the tram and stop looking out at the rich blue sea. At the tram stop, there are a dozen noisy teenagers flirting with each other in brightly coloured oversized clothes and you allow yourself a rueful smile and check the tram timetable.

Chapter 4

It is now six o'clock in the evening and the intensive heat has waned. The name of Michael Flannery's bar is called Osaka and is apparently a success. There are numerous groups of government workers and executives sipping their first post work cocktails in the late evening sun. The use of anything Japanese has been seen as refined and cultured for a number of years now.

The young man at the door with insufficient face hair to have let it grow, nods when you give your name and you're ushered in. The whole bar area is attractively sterile in the Japanese fashion. There are transparent seats and all tables are issued with small mock bonsai trees. The obese barmaid with shortly cropped auburn hair takes your order of straight vodka and nods back when you ask to speak to the owner.

It amuses you that most customers are slowly sipping on piping hot sake in oriental style shot glasses and most eating customers are awaiting what you know will be minute portions of fish gathered from a sea you stared out at this morning. The majority of the inhabitants are aged between twenty and thirty-five but are dressing consciously older. The clothes are influenced by the film actors of the mid twentieth century. Most females still have their hair neatly trimmed because of the heat but wear subtle frocks with thick leather belts and red high heels. The young men are wearing trousers cut high on the waist and some cover their heads in lightweight trilby hats.

A thin paper blind at the back of the bar is raised and the familiar face of Michael Flannery is revealed. He smiles and walks slowly towards you holding out his hand.

"You look well. How are you?" he enquires.

"I'm good, Mike. Nice place. Where do all the batteries go?"

You look up at all the bright neon lights surrounding the roof of the bar. Flannery gives you a generous grin back.

"Let's go upstairs smart arse. We can talk more freely there."

He then whispers in the ear of the barmaid and gestures for you to follow him.

Mike has always been known as 'Big Mike' and you are reminded why as you follow his silhouette up the stairs. He is well over six feet, broad shouldered, weighing about fifteen stone plus but without an ounce of fat on him. His balding head has been shaved neatly. The black shirt Mike is wearing looks painted on and makes him even more of an imposing figure. He's wearing expensive slim fit white trousers and black tassel loafers without socks. He's a good-looking man and looks every bit the successful businessman.

The apartment is immaculate and sparse with influences from the east everywhere. There are two light grey sofas aligned around an antique oak coffee table and you notice a large stone Buddha on top of a mock fireplace. All around the main room are framed pictures of ancient Japanese art with all windows covered by paper blinds. Mike has always been obsessed by Japan and you remember that he even worked there for a short time about a decade ago.

"Drink. I've just warmed up some sake?" He asks.

"Bourbon if you have it."

He smiles back and pours a neat large measure of bourbon into a thick-based crystal glass and you clink with his cup of sake before taking a generous sip. The bourbon is beautiful and you grin and slant your head in appreciation.

"I heard you'd landed on your feet," Mike says looking you up and down before he continues.

"You always were smarter than the others. It was only a matter of time before you grew up. The number of times I told you to get wise; running around with firecrackers playing war like kids."

You laugh back because anything Mike says is genuine and has no malice.

"You know why I'm here, Mike," you say seriously.

"They've got you looking for the kid?" he asks before you grimace and nod back.

"Well it makes sense. If anyone can slow that young fool down it's you. A few years locked up will do him some good," Mike predicts.

"They don't want him locked up, Mike," you say feeling your face contort. Mike moves two fingers across his neck.

"You mean?" He says and repeats the gesture.

"Yeah. He's pissed off the wrong people this time, Mike," you respond. His face has turned ashen but understands the situation

"So they've decided you're the man for the job, eh?" He enquires.

"I'm going to find him before they do. He needs to get out of the city. When did you last see him?" you ask coldly

Mike finishes off his drink and slowly nods his head and stares blankly then looks you in the eyes.

"He comes here a lot. He's usually with that idiot Mak and your mate Pete. What have you done to Mak? He can't stand the mention of your name."

He then grins at you ruefully and you smile back. Both of you know that he dislikes you after your thing with some blonde girl who Mak was soft on. It happened so long ago you can't remember her name.

"When were they last in Mike?"

"Must be a few weeks ago now. Old George was with them, drinking on an empty head as usual. I had to throw him out three nights ago. He never did know when to stop. The kid and Mak were going out of town for a few weeks."

"And Pete?" you ask sharply.

"Pete is still in the city. He was in last night with some brunette whom I've never seen before. She was no older than her late twenties. She was a pretentious sort and her arms were covered in tattoos of Karl Marx and 1950s film stars."

This amuses you because Pete has always been attracted to this type of girl, the pretentious idealist with dedicated opinions who'd see Pete as a mentor.

"Where is he staying?" you ask. Mike hesitates and walks over to a window and stares blankly at the sun setting on the coast.

"Mike?" he slowly turns round quickly to face you then speaks.

"Do you remember that bar we all used to go to years ago? The bloke who ran it would stay open for us once I'd finished on the door. All the regulars would get to stay and we'd all sit playing cards laughing till sunset. Do you remember?" He asks you with a vacant nostalgic look on his face.

"I remember. We'd still be drunk in the morning laughing at the commuters on the trams and do it all again. Things have to change though Mike and we're not young forever."

Mike has gone back to staring out of the window cradling his drink nodding his head slowly up and down in agreement. He turns back around and speaks again.

"Pete is staying at an upmarket beach apartment that Mak's cousin owns. Do you know the place?" He asks with an air of melancholy.

"Yes. Thank you, Mike," you say in sombre deference and put your empty glass on the oak coffee table. As you make your way to the exit Mike is still sipping sake watching the sunset and without turning round says.

"Try and let them leave the city. If you can't then just remember no one is forcing the kid and them to do these things."

"I'm just going to get them out Mike and that's all I want. Look after yourself, Big Mike," you say back earnestly.

As you leave Mike's apartment and make your way into the main bar you notice how busy it has become. The young doorman tilts his head as you leave and wishes you a good evening. There is a noisy group of girls in their early twenties surrounded by empty glasses and you walk past while they giggle. Then you wonder if the sickness in your stomach is down to Mike's expensive whiskey or because you know you've lied to an old friend.

Chapter 5

When you wake the next day your head is clear, you feel invigorated and prepared for a difficult day. Pete Baker was for a long time your closest friend in the cause. A shared twisted sense of humour and distrust of authority made you kindred spirits. The pair of you weren't enigmatic characters. If you'd worked hard on something during the day, then the evening would be dedicated to a few drinks, female company and having a laugh.

This was what you yearned for more than anything. It wasn't the thrill of an assignment but the evenings spent leisurely winding each other up and laughing uncontrollably that you missed. The work you did as a government observer wasn't uninteresting, it just lacked the common brotherhood that the cause encouraged. As young men Pete Baker and you could drink to the small hours of a morning and feel no ill effects the following morning.

For breakfast you have bacon on toast, squeezed orange juice and two mugs of tea. It is still not nine o'clock in the morning when you've put on your chocolate brown suit, white shirt and burgundy tie. The gun the government have issued you with, is perched in the side of your left shoulder; you slip on your black leather loafer shoes and leave the apartment.

The upmarket beach apartments are well known throughout the city and you even remember the government advertising campaign. At first the more affluent members of the city seemed hesitant to invest in the properties with an ever-changing coastal front and it was feared they would be adapted in to high-end capsule flats. Once this anxiety was relieved by an assurance that the apartments were mobile and could be moved backwards due to any coastal erosion the city elite sought them.

There are now well over fifty apartments and several restaurants, cafes and bars have been constructed around them. The largest of the restaurants is called Fuji Mountain and it is here that you are slowly sipping a black coffee and eating a chilled ice-cold ham sandwich. The restaurant is just less than fifty metres away from where Pete is staying and you've seen him leave the apartment twice. The first time he was bringing back what looked like milk, then three hours later he returned with a large bottle of scotch.

It was during Pete Baker's returning visit with the scotch that you suspected he'd seen you. The glance was brief and lasted barely a few seconds but it was the preceding double take that left you suspicious. He looked anxious for a few moments and then this quickly dissipated into what seemed like a fawn like grace. Baker shifted into an upright military position marching towards his apartment, entering it through the extended porch.

There have been three hours since the lights in the main room were switched off and only a dim light can be made from the back of the apartment. Pete Baker came out onto the porch with a glass of whiskey in hand. He stared out at the sea expressionless. It was only when the city's workforce began arriving home that he switched off the lights and appeared to retire for the evening.

The appearance of a stranger at the Fuji Mountain had gone largely unnoticed and you'd tipped generously in an obvious attempt to be left alone. Once the sun began to set on the gleaming sea you'd switched from coffee and pouring cream to large measures of bourbon. As you slowly sipped the drink you continued focusing on the apartment fifty metres in front of you.

It is only when the last light fades into darkness that you stand from your chair. The third waiter to serve you seems impressed with the money left and you raise your hand as a gesture of gratitude. A sea breeze brushes over your neatly cropped scalp cooling the sweat beads on the forehead.

As you approach the apartment you hear a distinct clicking noise and instinctively throw yourself onto the beach. To the left of you, a clump of wet sand leaps up into the air as if ripped from the ground falling onto the back of your head. There are small sections of beach metres away where the moonlight isn't reflecting and you slide towards one of them. Another lump of sand cascades up from the coast even closer to you than the last one but you feel triumphant when you find yourself in the shade.

It takes you only seconds to remove the government issued gun from inside your jacket and you fix your gaze on the pitch-black outline of the apartment waiting for the next shot to come from Pete Baker's silencer. The next shot is a good five metres from where you lay and you grin ruefully knowing that he has no idea where you've gone.

"We shouldn't be doing this you know!" your old friend cries out before laughing manically. It isn't that familiar repetitive cackle you remember of the man you clinked glasses with a thousand times. There is a nervous edge to it because he's vainly hoping you'll respond revealing your location. Instead he's inadvertently given you the advantage and you leap to your feet as best as possible in wet sand letting off four rounds from your gun in quick succession.

The final shot makes contact and you hear Pete scream out in agony. There are several people at the nearest restaurant that have heard the gunshots and it isn't long before they have redirected the main bar lights onto the beach. Pete has one hand held over his stomach, whilst the other is trying desperately to reach out for his silencer.

A young waitress with shaved bleached blonde hair who has seen him screams out widely covering her eyes.

"Step back, please madam. This is a government matter!" you forcefully state before timidly treading on the sand to stand over Pete. The gun is only inches from his left hand and there is desperation in Pete's face as he stretches out his fingers. This look fades when you kick away his weapon and look down with as much empathy as you can gather.

Pete Baker is losing blood from his stomach rapidly and his face is pale. The muscles in your back wrench as you crouch down and hold out your hand. He grabs it and looks up.

"You always were a lucky bastard." He grimaces at you.

"Why didn't you just keep your mouth shut, Pete?" you reply before smiling.

"I thought I might have you with one of my old tricks, you government men are pretty slow usually?" he replies before a sustained coughing fit.

The fourth bullet that left your gun has hit Pete on the left side of his stomach and exited the body on the same side. There are a couple of people who've ignored your instructions to stay back staring at him like he's in an exhibit. He may be unaware of his circumstances but you have seen enough gunshot wounds to know Pete Baker will be out of hospital in days. Unfortunately, moments before you can offer this assurance you hear the monotonous tones of Mr Poe.

"I must say this is excellent work, Sergeant!" he bellows over the beach. He is wearing the latest fluorescent white linen issued for government crime scenes and looks absurd with his trilby hat and unnecessary wooden cane. There are two trim young men wearing the same luminous outfits stood either side of Poe.

"There he is gentlemen. Take him away."

On these instructions both men pull Pete Baker roughly from the beach and drag him to a nearby government air-transporter.

"Good work, Sergeant. Don't worry he'll receive adequate medical provisions. That leaves only two now, sergeant."

"Two?" you ask despondently.

"Yes, William Dudek and Andrei Makowski." He prods on your left shoulder with his cane then follows the other men onto the air-transporter.

Chapter 6

It takes less than an hour to get home to the apartment. The first thing you do is drain off the night air sweat from your body with a five-minute cold shower. It's approaching midnight but you pour yourself a liberal measure of bourbon from the decanter on top of the bookcase, and reach for a photography book on 1950s Jazz.

As you turn through the pages of the smoke filled dimly lit bars, and faces of legendary musicians you've long since admired, you let your mind float for about half an hour. Then placing the book back on the shelf you pull up the paper blinds, loosen your tie and step out onto the balcony.

The heat is still incredible and you wipe your brow with a handkerchief noticing how the lights in the capsule quarters have already been switched off. The Department of Environmental Concern has been campaigning for citizens to save valuable resources. This hasn't stopped the more desirable areas of the city remaining ablaze with electrical lighting till 4 o'clock in the morning. Today has left you mentally exhausted and as a myriad of thoughts enter your mind you, decide on bed.

When you wake up, the dry humid air has cooled and it takes only ten minutes to leave the flat after two black coffees. The recently purchased three-piece navy suit is tailored and fits beautifully. When you tighten a woollen blue tie up to your pink cotton shirt and slip on some black tassel loafers you're in a good mood.

It's early enough to avoid most commuters and you relish the chance to be seated on the tram. The carriages are moving fast, which allows a welcome breeze to enter through the tram windows. In just under twenty minutes of travelling you have arrived at your destination, the Department of Counter Protection.

One of the young men who helped remove Pete from the beach yesterday is waiting outside the main door to the department and he grins at you insincerely holding out his hand. His palm is filled with sweat and you quickly withdraw.

"Colonel Poe has requested that I take you directly to our interrogation suites."

He states officiously, nervously patting down the sweat from his prematurely balding head. The reference to Poe's rank and the overly tight black linen suit that he's wearing make you smile. The young man leads you through several long queues of frustrated looking people holding documents. The two of you march through several checkpoints without having to show the relevant identification papers that you're carrying.

There are two guards stood either side of the entrance to the suites, both standing rigidly with stale expressions on their faces. The larger of the guards shakes your associates hand as the young man whispers into his ear gesturing towards you. The guard then nods gently in agreement and opens the door to the interrogation suites.

There can be no more than ten suites and only three have occupants. All of them are constructed with transparent glass, which lends a perverse antiseptic feeling to the place. As your guide exits you notice Pete in the suite furthest away from the entrance and you both make your way to a small crowd of officials outside what is now Peter Baker's prison cell.

There is a long white rectangular block attached to the side of the suite, which Pete Baker is now laid on. The exit wound has been tightly wrapped up in bandages with a small circular bloodstain in the middle. A slim attractive young woman is seated at a desk with a large laptop taking notes. In front of her standing outside Baker's cell are Poe and two studious looking officials.

"Good morning, Sergeant," says Poe without looking at you. His gaze is fixed firmly on Baker.

"Why does this man have no medical supervision sir?"

You ask politely as you can summon. Pete laughs softly then groans clutching his wound. The young official to the right of Poe appears perplexed.

"The man is an enemy of the state and has antecedents dating back two decades." This leaves you incensed but before you can respond Poe turns round placing his arm firmly on your shoulder.

"Mr Baker has received more than sufficient medical assistance sergeant. It is important that one remains objective in all parts of this investigation." His sickly smile leaves you cold, but you nod back in acknowledgement. The elder of the two officials hits the window of the cell.

"Get up!" He bellows. Pete uses his right arm to prop himself into an upright position, grimacing as he does so. When he is seated upright you notice severe bruising on his right cheekbone and he has a deep cut above the left eyebrow. The mischievous grin and look of comradeship that an injured Pete Baker showed yesterday has gone. His bloodshot eyes are now filled with hatred.

The official to Poe's left steps forward staring at Baker intensely.

"It is in your best interests to cooperate with us fully, Mr Baker." Pete remains silent as the official continues,

"It is exceedingly important that we locate a Mr Andrei 'Mak' Makowski and one William 'Kid' Dudek. We believe that you can assist in our investigation Mr Baker."

The pompous way the official speaks seems to amuse him. He fixes his gaze on you and smirks ruefully.

"Did you hear that? This young man says it's exceedingly important. In that case I will have to be exceedingly cooperative." Pete's question is rhetorical and you nod back reassuringly before he continues,

"Unfortunately, I've never heard of either of those gentlemen. What time is tea served here? I'm very hungry." This makes you smile before stepping closer to Pete's cell to plead with him.

"Come on, Pete, you know how this works. These people need information, which I know you have. In exchange for that you could be a citizen again in five years." Pete moves closer to the glass and replies,

"That's a beautiful suit you're wearing. It must be pleasant being able to afford the finer things in life. I heard you had a spacious new apartment. I can picture all the Japanese art and immaculately framed film posters. You always were a pretentious prick. How do you work with these people?" Any empathy you had for your Pete evaporates.

"I'm not the one covered in blood, standing in a transparent prison cell Pete." He smiles ruefully then replies,

"Why did you do it?"

It would be cathartic to explain to Pete Baker the reasons why you joined the government. One reason was to end the horrific beatings the officials handed out in the interrogation room. Pete would probably understand that the threats made concerning your brother were what finally helped you rationalise the betrayal. However it's much easier to turn your back on him and walk away.

"Good luck, Pete," you say softly. Poe whispers conspiratorially in the ear of one of the officials and you make your way to the exit. As you open the door you hear him bellow,

"You Bastard!" It takes you nearly 50 minutes to work your way through the departmental paper work and identity checks before you are on the street. The intensity of the heat has increased and you seek shelter in a small bar called 'Rick's Place'. The paintwork inside is peeling and the film pictures on the wall look faded. A barmaid who looks too young to be working there asks what you'd like. She pours you a small measure of scotch.

The bar is entirely barren apart from a tired looking elderly man cradling a beer in the far corner. The scotch tastes dreadful and you sip it slowly. Poe's plan that your presence might make Pete more lucid has failed and you try unsuccessfully to remove the image of Pete Baker being tortured by the officials.

Chapter 7

In the morning you rise early and have two black coffees with some bacon on toast. The temperature has noticeably dropped and you put on slim fitting cream trousers, a white cotton shirt and navy umpire jacket. The suede brown loafers you chose last night are sitting neatly near the door. The red tie selected yesterday remains on a side table and you slip your bare feet into the shoes before leaving. The trams to the central station run regularly and it takes less than five minutes for one to arrive.

It is surprisingly quiet when you arrive at the station, and you purchase a return ticket without queuing. The sun is now shining through the transparent roof and a handful of cleaners are applying mops to the gleaming black surface of the station. The back pages of the paper are dominated by the sacking of the National Football coach, which you estimate is the fifth dismissal in two years. If the position wasn't so over paid, you ponder; no one would apply for such a precarious job.

It has been years since you've followed any sport, your favourite Cricket was rendered obsolete decades ago, once players began passing out through heat exhaustion. The government then banned daytime football six years ago and even tried to increase the length of half time so players could recover from the humidity. This was an irrelevance to you, since you had long since realised that these pastimes were created to distract us all from the mess the world is in. The train you're now sitting on slowly moves out and that last idealistic thought makes you smile as you stare out at the coast.

This journey should take no longer than an hour, followed by a fifteen-minute walk. The destination has no official title or place on a map and the selected few who know it call it Sanctuary.

His story was that he'd been a middle ranking civil servant in an obscure foreign posting in India. The job was to relay information about pharmaceutical companies and make sure they followed strict guidelines based on the Globalisation and Environment Act. It was years later that he told you he could tolerate the sterile administrative duties that were part of his remit, because he was learning so much about himself.

He was recalled home after a three-year stint, but it didn't take long for him to decide to return to India. The people of his homeland seemed alien to him, asleep but with their eyes open he'd always say. In India he devoted himself to learning various techniques of meditation, living in the moment and finding joy in the small but beautiful things in life. After five years of travelling, just as his savings began to run out he received a message that his Uncle had died and instantly knew this meant he'd inherited a small fortune.

Once he arrived home, began an immediate search for a secluded area on the outskirts of the city he'd once worked in. A perfect location was found and purchased somewhere on the coast sixty miles north of the city. The construction of Sanctuary took six months and half of his inheritance.

It's five minutes after stepping off the train when you see a collection of undistinguishable figures walking on the distant coastline. Upon arriving at the Sanctuary you are touched by a faint nostalgia. The wooden meditation temples have faded from the sun, but still have an understated beauty.

A youthful couple sitting on the beach look up at you, both smiling.

"Hey. How are you mate?" asks the young man. He is wearing mid twentieth century style sky blue swimming shorts, which have a taper round the middle. He is shirtless and suntanned; his eyes riddled red by the drugs laid next to the right of his female associate.

"I'm fine young man," you say smiling back generously, feeling self-conscious in two layers of clothes. The grandest of the temples is in the centre of the beach. After removing the umpire jacket and placing it over your right shoulder you notice the entrance to the temple. On your way across the white sand you turn back and notice two young couples running into the sea naked laughing uproariously. This makes you smile and reflect on times you've spent here.

When you turn round he is stood upright staring directly into your eyes. He holds out his hand.

"It's been a long time since you've visited my humble abode." You shake his hand firmly. He's wearing luminous white linen trousers and a loose fitted short-sleeved pale blue shirt. His hair has thinned prodigiously and is now completely white rather than grey. The hair is neatly trimmed and still spiked upwards despite the sparseness.

"I've got my health, Chris," you say confidently. He must be in his early seventies and looks tremendous. The skin is tanned but healthy and the stark blue eyes stand out in the approaching midday sun.

"Please let us go inside. The heat can sometimes be quite intense." He extends his hand in a gesture towards his temple entrance. The cool air inside tempers the beads of sweat on your shaved head.

The main room is sparsely lit and furnished as you remembered. At the back of the right hand side of the room is a tethered light grey sofa with a luxuriant footstool opposite. There is nothing on the walls, but the few bookshelves are covered in framed Japanese art and Buddhist icons. There has been no glass instilled in the window frames, and the paper blinds attached blow gently in the wind.

A large expensive cream mattress dominates the back of the room with a small navy pillow rested firmly on top. He has already retired to another room and returns with a bottle of twelve-year-old scotch.

"I need to talk to you about something, Chris," you insist. He looks at you calmly and nods slowly.

"You don't need to do anything, but I suggest you have a large glass of this." He fills your glass with a generous portion of scotch and you dutifully pour it down your neck.

"I don't like having to do this Chris," you say before he holds up his hand gesturing you to be silent.

"Why don't you rest here?" he says looking towards the cream mattress. He pours you another drink, which you dispose of immediately, before staring up sympathetically.

"I'm sorry Chris, but I must ask you some questions you won't like." He smiles and replies,

"The answers for these questions can be broached tomorrow," he then pours the largest of the three drinks he's offered you. The room feels so serene that you decide to have a brief moment on the luxuriant mattress, whilst you drink it.

The alcohol has reduced the anxiety and fear, but years of experience signify that this is a short-term plan. The feelings you felt this morning were almost unbearable. It was nigh impossible to removes the cinematic images of you friend Peter Baker in agony.

"Why don't you get some sleep?" asks Chris in a slow soothing voice before adjusting the navy pillow so you can rest your head on the soft silk.

"They have, Pete," you groan.

He again raises his arm in a gesture of peace and then nods reassuringly.

"I caught him, Chris. I shot him in the dark. I can't do this." You follow this with a childish sigh.

In five minutes, sleep takes you on a soft mattress and comfortable pillow. Unfortunately, during the sleep you dream of Pete Baker's inevitable death through brutal interrogation.

Chapter 8

When you wake up for the first time you notice night has descended. There are several incense candles strategically placed round the room. Chris is crouched outside the temple entrance, hovering over a dimly lit stove. He is slowly stirring a pot with a large wooden spoon. The steam is rising into the night air when Chris turns round and notices you have risen. He pours the pot into an ample sized china mug.

'Sake' Chris gently pushes you back on the mattress and allows you to slowly sip the contents. It tastes delicious and you lean back on to your right shoulder. The white haired old man then places a navy blanket over the mattress and you fall into a blissful sleep.

It is a distinct smell of bacon that wakes you in the morning and you can see Chris using the stove from last evening to slowly cook several rashers. The full quota of rest leaves you euphoric and you slowly walk to the sunlit temple entrance. He looks up from the stove.

"I've made coffee," Chris is pointing to a large blackened pot covered by an equally dark lid.

"Thank you, but I'm going for a swim," you reply and he nods knowingly.

"There are some bathing shorts inside the temple if you've become bashful in your old age," he asks and you smile back at the blue eyes before turning to the sea. The sand doesn't feel warm on your bare feet and dawn was less than two hours ago.

Once in the water you are jolted awake by the briskness, which recedes after a few rapid breaststrokes through the calm morning sea. It seems less than half an hour before the arms and shoulders feel suitably tired. When drying the body down you notice the distinct scar on your left shoulder. The neat signature left by a French surgeon after an unpleasant road accident. A daily swim was suggested to restore muscle strength and flexibility. These exercises left you feeling just as you do now, awake and mindful.

At the temple Chris is seated outside meditating. The legs are crossed and both hands placed on the knees. His posture is dignified and his eyes are closed. When you first saw him meditating you were left dumbfounded and cynical. It seemed alien to your upbringing, but after a few visits Chris had both the kid and you sat upright surrounded by incense candles. He told you both to try stay in the moment. This is when Mak marched off nodding his head sideways laughing.

He opens his eyes and points to two mugs of green tea placed on the thin pine desk. The teas are piping hot and after taking a small sip you raise the mug in gratitude. Chris pushes himself up from the floor and stretches his neck from left to right.

"They have you looking for the Kid?" He asks casually letting his blue eyes meet you. The question disrupts your calmed mind and you answer back sharply.

"Yes. It's a question of survival, Chris."

He looks back at you placidly, removing a small piece of loose threading from his linen trousers.

"I'm not judging you. I would always avoid that, it's just that you seemed very anxious last night," Chris replies quietly. The serene qualities of Chris encourage you to raise your hand and nod your head apologetically.

"I'm sorry, Chris. I didn't mean to snarl at you, it feels like I've no way out of this." He smiles generously and beckons you to sit with him outside the temple.

"The kid was here about a week ago," he states clearly before looking at you for a response.

"Alone?" you enquire coldly.

"He was with some young girl, Mak too. Mak spent the three days drinking whiskey and trying to antagonise anyone in a ten yard radius." This makes you smile and you gesture for Chris to continue.

"Mak has no love for you anymore. He thinks you've betrayed them all just to stay alive. The kid was more difficult to read. He spent days meditating with me whilst the girl swam and Mak drank."

"No mention of me from the kid?" you enquire.

"If your name was mentioned Mak began swearing and became violent. He put his foot through one of the temple windows and threw a bottle of whiskey at a young couple," Chris says despondently. This information is titular and you raise your eyebrows at Chris regarding the kid.

"When your name was mentioned to the kid he'd just smile and walk off. He spent hours strolling along the coast staring out at the sea."

"Where's the kid now?" you ask sharply. Chris puts his hands through his thin white hair and looks up to the rich blue sky.

"I don't know. The kid and Mak went their separate ways after the three days. Mak said he was going to stay at his cousin's place further along the coast."

This information ignites a distant memory and you recall meeting Mak's cousin four years ago before a mission.

"Aron?" you ask with more courtesy than your last enquiry. Chris runs his finger across his thin white hair deep in contemplation, before nodding his head slowly in agreement. Aron was younger than Mak by at least a decade. He was slim with pin like eyes and a hawkish nose. There was none of Mak's aggressive nature but Aron was equally repellent. He would linger on his cousin's every word and you grimace in memory of that sycophantic laugh.

"Aron's place is five miles north of here. There are a handful of two storey flats overlooking the coast. They are popular holiday homes; I think they've just finished building a new bar next to the shops," Chris states calmly. There is no possibility of Chris telling you the whereabouts of the Dudek, even if he knew.

"Thank you, Chris," you hold out your hand, which he shakes dutifully.

"I hope you're not going to rush off. You're more than welcome to stay another night," Chris politely offers. It seems ungrateful to decline and you agree to stay.

After another hour-long swim in the placid sea you feel serene and content. Chris senses you desire space, and you sunbathe appreciatively letting your mind float. In the evening he's prepared a banquet. The freshly fried fish tastes sublime and you indulge as freely as your appetite allows. Chris ensures that your glass never remains devoid of his finest scotch. The sun hasn't set before you decide to let sleep take you.

In the morning you rise early and notice Chris is already awake meditating towards the rose painted skyline. It seems imprudent to disturb him and you decide to make your way back to the tram stop. The heat's intensity is tamed by a sea breeze that sweeps away the sweat beads from your head.

At the station you purchase a ticket for 'New Kyoto' and wince at the pretentiousness of the names given to new settlements. It's still only approaching seven o'clock in the morning so the tram is nearly empty. The journey takes just under twenty minutes to reach your latest destination.

The station sign at 'New Kyoto' looks immaculate and has a picture of a young family. The father and mother are both dressed in swimming clothes pointing their children to the sea line. It's the inane look on the father's face that makes you grin as you make your way down the newly constructed platform steps.

A gust of breeze gently blows sand onto the steps as you make your descent. There are four two-storey apartments about a hundred metres from the incoming tide. On the left of these cream painted apartments is an array of shops. Then on the adjacent side is a bar that appears to be opening.

Chapter 9

In the distance you glance a middle-aged man in lightweight sports clothes running along the coast. He speeds past the buildings and shops and you notice he's wearing a white headband, already drenched in sweat. The prospect of intense physical exertion before you've had breakfast makes you wince. The newly constructed bar is called 'Aqua Bar Café' with just one occupant. An angelic faced boy no older than nineteen is sitting in an acrylic red chair sipping tea. He's obviously the waiter that you saw opening up for business.

"Hello, could I get a table please?" you ask genially. He steps up languidly gesturing that the ten remaining bar tables are at your disposal.

"I'll just get you a menu sir," he says courteously. The young man then returns holding one leather-bound menu.

"I'd like a large mug of black coffee, wheat toast, scrambled eggs and well done bacon please." The piping hot coffee is refreshing, and the eggs taste delicious. A handful of bacon rashers have been cooked as requested and your breakfast leaves you revitalised.

It is still barely 8.30am when you leave the bar having left a generous tip. The coastline looks radiant and you slip off your loafers and walk along the tide. The ice-cold sea feels soothing on your bare feet and you wander up and down the tide for the next 45 minutes. When you return to the settlement there is more activity in the shops and you notice one of the apartment blocks is actually a hotel.

The entrance to the hotel has a bulky man stood imposingly at the top of the five large steps. He is wearing a slim fit black linen suit and on his head is a wide brimmed fedora hat. The neatly dressed man touches the left of his hat and bows respectively.

"Good morning, sir," he says politely and you smile back in recognition.

There is an auburn haired woman behind the hotel's reception. The sporadic grey hairs have left her hair looking dull and her thin lips and beady eyes seem hostile.

"Hello. I'd like a single room for the evening," you say feigning all the courtesy you can muster.

"We are extremely busy at present sir. It would be better if you'd have booked in advance."

Her lips curl as she raises her eyebrows conspiratorially. It annoys you, but you take your government identification card and place it on the reception desk.

"I do apologise, Sergeant. I'm sure we can accommodate a government official. There is a room available on the ground floor, it has an en suite bathroom and a view of the sea," she informs you.

"That sounds perfect," you reply sardonically and take the digital key she offers.

The room is spacious but humid and you open both large windows. On the table you place a small bottle of whiskey before pouring yourself a generous measure into a hotel plastic glass. After three large drinks of this whiskey you lay on the hotel bed and let sleep take its course.

It is nearly eight in the evening; you walk to the bathroom and splash cold water onto your face. There is more commotion now and you can hear female laughter outside. When glancing through the room window you notice a young couple flirting on the beach. He has neatly shorn blonde hair and is whispering into the olive skinned girl's ear. She responds by giggling and thrusting the boy away before pulling him back.

The hotel lobby is a short walk from the room and you nod politely at the receptionist still standing behind a desk. She smiles back suspiciously and squints her eyes.

"Have a pleasant evening, Sergeant," she says watching your movements with an unusual intensity. It is eerily quiet outside the hotel and the only sounds are the tides coming in and distant chatter in the café.

Then suddenly you hear a rapid succession of footsteps and feel a blow to the back of the neck that knocks you to your knees. It is the surprise rather than the ferocity of the attack that dumbfounds you. When rising gingerly to your feet you hear a grating high-pitched laugh.

"You should stay down!" shrills the attacker.

"Hello, Aron," you remark, relieved to see he is unaccompanied by his brother. Aron can't be in his thirties yet and his jet-black hair is spiked up in a dishevelled style. It's obvious that the receptionist has informed Aron of your arrival.

"Come on then!" he yells before swinging a punch that misses your head by a clear yard. The momentum from this failed effort leaves him unsteady and you quickly thump him twice in the stomach. He groans as you follow this with a succession of strikes to the face. The last of these punches sends Aron Makowski crashing onto the beach.

He's unconscious when you attach braces to the wrists and turn him over so his bloodied face isn't in the sand. You remove the government tracker from your belt and call in a Code NOV78. He begins opening his eyes when the Security Helicopter descends onto the beach, and you see a stark look of apprehension on the ashen face.

"Up you get," you say dragging Aron to his feet. There are two government officials who climb out of the helicopter onto the beach. The pilot salutes you, which you find unnerving. The taller of the men then starts to usher away a small crowd of people gathering round the helicopter. The pilot is a stout man with grey hair at the temples and has a flattened nose. He efficiently guides Aron into the Security vehicle attaching a safety belt over his new prisoner. The helicopter then takes flight towards the city lights in the distance. You asked them to intern him in a basic offender cell. There is no need to involve the blunt technique of the government interrogators.

In ten minutes you're at the Aqua bar cradling a drink and replaying the events of today in your mind. The reckless way you announced yourself at the hotel was dangerous and stupid. This mistake could have been fatal if it had been Mak who'd spoken to the receptionist and not his brother. It was definitely the receptionist who'd informed of your arrival to New Kyoto.

"Another drink, sir?" asks the waitress. She is wearing a green blouse which clashes with the red chairs scattered round the restaurant.

"Yes, please," you remark handing her twenty Euros. The whiskey tastes delicious and by the time you order a third drink any anxiety has dissipated. It seems like a sensible idea though to head back to the city after the fourth large measure is poured.

On the tram home you notice how most passengers are asleep, whether this is through exhaustion or abuse you don't speculate. The later trains always have the destitute slumped in corners of the tram. They've made the correct assumption that the government officials in charge of ticket inspection have retired for the evening. A civil servant from a department you've long since forgotten once told how the ticket administrators were content for vagrants to slum after midnight.

When you get to the apartment you're physically and mentally exhausted. There is a minimum amount of alcohol left in the decanter and you pour this into one of the thick-based crystal glasses. You turn the pages of a book on meditation before stretching out on the sofa.

After falling asleep for a couple hours you are woken by the sunrise. The paper blinds fall down quickly when you remove the pegs that hold them aloft. The clock says just past five in the morning and your mind is still racing. There is no noise outside when you open the largest of the apartment windows. It's going to be another challenging day so you decide on at least two hours of sleep in a bed.

Chapter 10

It is a relatively cool day and you decide to wear your navy wide brimmed fedora hat. When you arrive at the main offender centre it's a few minutes past nine and it's raining. Aron is in cell 41 and a pleasant government corporal politely escorts you there. He's hunched over the wooden chair situated at the rear of all offender blocks, with his head in his hands. As you enter the cell Aron looks up and you notice the dark bruising on his right cheekbone.

"Hello Aron, did you get a good night's sleep?" you ask sarcastically. He wipes tears away from his eyes and you grin back sadistically. Aron looks pathetically impotent in his ill-advised fashion conscious clothes. The tight white trousers are now stained in sand and dirt. His beige shirt is loose fitted and covered in sporadic bloodstains. Aron's suede loafers are a luminous orange in the latest style.

"You're in a lot of trouble young man," you say trying to illicit a response.

"I'm not the only one you shit!" he barks back.

"That might be the case Aron, but I'm not the one covered in blood wiping tears away. Unless you cooperate with me I will personally make sure you spend the rest of your useless existence in a room just like this. I might even ensure you get a roommate to keep you company," you reply menacingly. He begins weeping into his hands and you relax in the knowledge that this interrogation will be simple.

"I don't want to do that though Aron. All I'd like to know is when you last saw your brother," you say with more sympathy.

"If I tell you I can go?" he whimpers.

"Immediately," you reply with authority.

He nods his head from left to right and rolls his eyes before beginning his confessional. In between his relentless crying and

47

incoherent rambling he tells you that Mak's staying at the place of some woman called Sarah.

"Sarah Booth?" you ask him.

"Yes, that's her. She lives in the 'Seven Sisters' apartments?" he answers raising his head. The 'Sisters' are a group of five storey flats with luminous pink window frames in every apartment. The flats have been called 'Seven Sisters' since construction finished ten years ago.

"Can I leave now?" he asks. The tears and bloodstained clothes merged together leave Aron looking like a stray dog.

"I'll certainly do my best Aron," you reply earnestly.

It takes a small gesture to the corporal that you've finished for him to guide you to the exit.

"I'm much obliged corporal. Please keep him for a couple of hours. This would be greatly appreciated by my department. If he causes any of you problems use your own discretion," you inform the diligent inferior. He salutes and you pace out into the late morning air.

It is still a mild day and you put your fedora back on once outside. There are gentle raindrops hitting the top of the hat and you smile as one slowly slips down the brim. The encounter with Mak's brother leaves you feeling anxious and it takes only five minutes to find a suitable bar. After ordering a large measure of bourbon with no ice you take a seat outside the bar and people watch. When you're drinking the second drink the crowds of people going for their dinner become noticeably larger.

The majority of people are wearing the newly fashionable waterproof ponchos. The colours are variable; the younger generation adopt brash luminous green and yellow overcoats, whereas the older citizens wear brown, grey and navy waterproofs. After your fourth order of whiskey you decide to postpone the visit to the 'Seven Sisters' until tomorrow. You raise yourself from your chair and begin the walk to the tram stop with as much dignity as you can fathom.

Sarah Booth has been Mak's girlfriend for over a decade and blames every one of his associates for his predicament. Mak has been misled, misunderstood and led astray by the kid, Pete, you and anyone else she can recall.

"Please stay a little longer, Sergeant." The voice is familiar and you turn back looking over your left shoulder. Poe is patting his sweat-ridden forehead with a sky blue handkerchief and makes a polite gesture towards one of the white chairs. Poe then gets the attention of an adolescent waiter by waving his right hand extravagantly.

"What can I get you sir?" the waiter enquires dutifully.

"I'll have a large glass of beer please." Poe then stares at you waiting for a response.

"Can I get a whiskey please, young man?" you reply looking at the waiter sympathetically. He returns with both drinks in under five minutes and Poe hands him a crisp twenty-Euro note.

"I must confess to enjoying these milder days Sergeant. The constant heat and humidity make it difficult to think. I'm old enough to remember when it still snowed."

He is wearing an ill-fitting double-breasted black suit, with a cream shirt and navy tie.

"What do you want?" you ask curtly. He lowers his large frame into the chair, taken aback by your abruptness.

"It would help if you didn't see me as an enemy. I am here to offer you any assistance that you require. There are esteemed members of the government who are most pleased with your progress," he responds diplomatically.

"Why are you following me?" you ask in an aggressive tone. Poe winces before nodding his head in mock disapproval.

"Do you think that a man with your colourful background and catalogue of antecedents will be permitted free rein?"

He raises his eyebrows and waits for your recognition. You look back at him with a sardonic grin and reply,

"It's just that I would prefer to work alone on this case sir." He sits up in his chair pointing his finger at you enthusiastically.

"The government understands that entirely Sergeant!" he bellows before lowering his volume and continuing.

"We would simply like reassurance that as the case extends to its natural conclusion, the government is kept informed. Once William Dudek is located you'll require assistance," the eyebrows are raised again.

"I understand, sir," you state subserviently.

He takes a small sip from the glass and stares lecherously as an attractive female commuter walks past your table. Poe wipes sweat from his thick neck using the sky blue handkerchief and then continues.

"Did you have a productive talk with young Mr Makowski?"

"An informative discussion sir, I'll be investigating a new lead in the morning," you reply as politely as can be managed. Then he replies instantly,

"Sarah Booth of Seven Sisters, E Block, second floor, flat 16." Poe's eyes narrow and he grins at you ruefully. He has the appearance of a man who has just revealed a winning hand in a game of cards.

"What colour is the door sir?" you state with mock sincerity.

"Just make sure everything is in the report Sergeant. If you locate Andrei Makowski do not attempt to arrest him alone." The sinister smile has evaporated and he's risen to his feet.

"Yes sir," you reply looking disapprovingly at Poe's choice of brown brogues.

"Well, keep up the good work Sergeant. Please try not to drink too much this evening." He then puts on his wide brimmed black hat and strolls out of the bar. You get the attention of the waiter.

"Same again please, young man."

Chapter 11

It is nearly 7 o'clock in the morning when you wake with a vague recollection of when you retired to bed. The hangover is acute and you relieve the symptoms with a large glass of ice-cold water. In a few minutes you feel more relaxed and return to your bed, where you sleep till just before 10 o'clock.

You are showered and dressed in half an hour and having glanced outside the window before deciding to wear your cream linen suit, sky blue shirt and brown suede loafers. After two large coffees, bacon on toast and a glass of freshly squeezed orange juice you make your way to the nearest tram stop.

The tram is almost entirely barren and includes just a few pensioners and a dishevelled younger woman clutching a battered and worn hip flask with tweed on both sides. She smiles at you, revealing a missing front tooth then murmurs incomprehensively. Nodding back sympathetically you undo the button on your jacket and begin reading one of the countless free newspapers scattered on the tram seats.

The front page is dominated by the story of a seven year old that has raised 10,000 Euros for charities by swimming five miles. On the back pages is an image of a mud soaked football pitch, flash floods making last night's game almost unplayable.

It is barely past nine o'clock in the morning when you arrive at the nearest tram stop to the 'Seven Sisters', outside the station are half a dozen bars and restaurants. The most frequented one is a faux Irish themed pub; with a collection of early drinkers all cradling their pints like vulnerable infants. The three adjacent restaurants have luminous acrylic tables, with plain chairs pointed towards the now bright morning sun.

In these dull coloured chairs are seated a mixed group of about ten men and women in their early twenties. You take a seat opposite this group and order a large black coffee. An extravagantly dressed young man is dominating the conversation, switching from topics as diverse as politics to his misadventures the previous evening. He is wearing a white linen flat cap, burgundy braces over a sky blue shirt with the top button done up with no tie. Draped over his chair is a thick tweed jacket, that seems an odd choice considering the humidity. Most strikingly of all are the light pink cotton socks he's wearing underneath the shiniest penny loafers you can recollect seeing.

All of the males have grown long unkempt beards, and the varying degrees of success in these endeavours make you smile. The females are no less inconspicuous in their appearances. The young ladies are wearing Breton tops of different shades and red and navy scarves tightly wrapped round their thin necks. The female getting most of the attention is wearing a pale blue Japanese style kimono with wooden clogs. You people watch for about forty minutes slowly sipping two coffees. It is possible to make out the distinct window frames of the 'Sisters' building about half a mile into the distance. After paying for your drinks, you slowly rise up and iron out any creases in your suit with both hands.

The 'Sisters' district used to be where the Eastern bloc migrants were housed when you were growing up; there are still remnants of this world if one looks, the Polish graffiti on the 'snicket' walls, offshoots of the different roads. You notice a derelict vodka bar with faded window blinds and rust laden chairs outside.

It was about ten years ago that an ambitious Government Minister decided to invest heavily in the district. Apparently, the land was cost effective and it took less than eighteen months to transform the area. The 'Seven Sisters' apartments were designed to encourage an eclectic but affluent group to move to the area. You remember the successful advertising campaign that convinced homosexuals, bohemian young professionals and small businesses of the benefits to living in such a vibrant place. Continental style cafes increasingly replaced the Irish pubs, with framed pictures from French cinema and canvas images of the newly built cities in China. The largely Polish migrants couldn't afford the now astronomical rental prices and moved out to the cramped capsule flats.

The 'Sisters' apartments are still impressive despite the influence of the sun on the now faded paint on most front doors. All the seven blocks are distinguishable and you follow the signs to 'E Block' giving a friendly nod as you pass two young men walking their dog along the path leading from the first set of flats. You press the small red button marked 'E Block: 1st Floor Apartment 2.

"Hello? John is that you? You're early. I thought we'd arranged for later on this evening for some food," an elderly female voice comes through the speaker outside the block. The voice is clear but annoyed.

"I'm terribly sorry about this but I'm not John. I've just moved in on the third floor, and have brought the key to my old apartment. In know this is a pain but would you mind…" Before you can finish your request the electronically controlled hall door slides open from left to right.

"Thank you," you politely say towards the speaker. There is no reply and you make your way inside to the ground floor. You grin ruefully at the ease in which you have entered the building. Perhaps in areas like these everyone is deemed trustworthy or more likely the individual who let you in simply doesn't care.

The ground floor entrance has little décor except for three large artificial plants neatly placed opposite the stairs. As you begin the ascent to the second floor you notice how the whole building feels antiseptic. The immaculate acrylic front doors of all the apartments are white. The floors are a mixture of glass and wooden panels. This gives the building the feeling of a newly constructed hospital with no patients. After a short walk up the stairs you knock firmly on last door on the left of the corridor, number 16. It startles you how quickly the door opens.

"What are you selling?" she asks with a contorted face.

"How are you, Sarah?" you ask sincerely. Sarah Booth looks visibly different, the blue-eyed innocence of the teenage barmaid rendered obsolete. The short-cropped peroxide hair is now shoulder length, with shades of silver grey protruding through the centre parting. Her complexion is pale and there are noticeable wrinkles round the eyes. She looks you up and down studiously, then nods disapprovingly at your attire.

"He isn't here," she says before rubbing your suit between her thumb and index finger.

"I'd like to come in," you state assertively. Her breath is fresh and she is wearing a reasonably expensive white kimono. Unfortunately, she can't hide her jaundiced eyes and tendency to sway to the left. On the middle shelf of the bookcase is a silver-plated hipflask. There are minute beads of sweat slithering down her forehead with an aroma you know to be associated with vodka. It is barely midday, but it requires no deductive logic to conclude that Sarah Booth is drunk.

The flat is immaculate and you can see the sheen glimmering off the glass coffee table, situated between two silver grey sofas with burgundy cushions. After picking up one of these cushions you take a seat. Sarah slower meanders to the hip flask and pours herself a large glass of vodka.

"Can I offer you a drink?" she asks. You squint your eyes and nod your head from left to right.

"That's not why I'm here, Sarah."

"I know why you're here you stuck up bastard!" Sarah yells with red-faced intensity. Then sits on the sofa opposite and after rubbing her temples a few times sits up in a more dignified position.

"What do you want to know?" she asks coldly.

Chapter 12

The view from Sarah's apartment window looks beautiful in the early afternoon light. There are already members of the workforce sitting outside indulging in an early lunch. In the distance it's possible to see dark outlines of people walking on the expansive coastline. The tide is out and you can just make out the sun reflecting on the ocean.

"Where is Mak?" you ask quietly, still staring out at the city landscape. She erupts into laughter, then points her unsteady index finger at you.

"That's what's funny. You won't believe me when I tell you!" Her laughter now has become more manic.

"Where is he?" You ask sternly.

"After all the things he said about them. He used to make jokes about them all." The shrill laughter continues and you finally lose your patience.

"Where is he?" you bark, now standing over her.

"Mak's found religion," Sarah Baker's amusement has now dissipated and you stare back in mild shock.

"He said he'd always felt a void in his life and was seeking more answers. Then about three days ago he vanished," she informs you. You motion for her to continue using your hand.

"All his stuff is in our room still. Can you believe it? Does this sound like Mak?" She pleads.

"Where is he, Sarah?" You ask for the final time, in a calm dispassionate tone.

"He's gone to one of those Buddhist retreats on the coast. It's costing him a small fortune. I've got the location written down; he wanted me to let him know if I needed any money. Well he can stuff his money," she rants triumphantly.

Sarah then pours what seem to be the final contents of her hipflask and hands you a small business card.

"It's called Sunset Meditation Retreat. The nearest tram stop and directions are on the back of the card. Now piss off and leave me alone."

When you reach the apartment door you turn back to thank Sarah, but she's already left the main room, probably to seek out more vodka. On the way downstairs you glimpse at the design of the card. It's beige, with the navy print that stands out because none of the words have capital letters. There is simple image of a sunset in the left hand corner. On the other side you read through the smudged writing she's added with a fountain pen.

There is a small quiet café nearby, with only three tables outside, and you take a seat in one of the feather light pine chairs. After ordering a large coffee with pouring cream you remove a five inch long cigar from the inside pocket of your linen jacket. A red-faced man in his late forties returns with the order and smiles dutifully placing a paper container of cream next to your coffee. You empty the contents and stir slowly, reflecting on Sarah's revelation about Mak.

The air is humid and it takes seconds to light the cigar. It has a sweet taste, and you blow out the smooth smoke calming your racing mind. The spiritual enlightenment of Mak doesn't surprise you to the same extent it has with Sarah. For the past two decades there has been an increase in meditation centres, relaxation retreats and various companies dedicated to eradicating modern day anxiety.

As Church attendances decreased with each passing year, this search for inner peace became a billion Euro dollar industry. You even remember the introduction of meditation suites in your final few years at school. Students would be ushered into the soundproof room every Wednesday afternoon, and a member of teaching staff demanding silence before playing Buddhist chanting through load speakerphones.

It was the kid that suggested visiting the Sanctuary and you were pleasantly surprised with the impact of a few days relaxation. Exposure to sea air and brisk morning swims always left you feeling serene. The thought of Mak sat with his legs crossed, breathing through his nose makes you smile.

"Enjoying your cigar, Sergeant?" says Poe. His considerable frame is squeezed into a pair of black linen trousers, held up by dark leather braces. Poe's white cotton shirt is drenched with sweat and a brown knitted tie hangs over his protruding stomach. The face is contorted by his huge teeth-bearing grin.

"Yes sir," you reply.

"Well you've definitely earned some brief rest bite. We are most pleased with the speed and progress of the investigation," he continues smiling inanely and takes a seat opposite.

"That's very gratifying, sir," you say dryly. This sense of pride in his voice makes you feel nauseous.

"I've been instructed to inform you that if there is anything you require, simply ask me. This comes from the highest authority Sergeant."

"I think it's probably best that I continue the investigation alone," you reply politely.

"We agree whole heartily, Sergeant. How has the investigation gone today?" His smile has receded and been replaced with a pensive frown. You place the card with Sarah's notes on the table in front of Poe.

"He's there," you say confidently pointing your finger over the address.

"William Dudek?" he enquires. It's quite obvious that he understands you mean Mak but you respond professionally.

"Andrei Makowski. Sarah Booth assures me that he can be found at this location. If I can find him, then I can find the main target."

"Quite. How do you intend to proceed, Sergeant?"

"I'll go there late in the morning, it doesn't seem like he's going anywhere."

"How do you intend to apprehend Mr Makowski when you find him? I can't imagine him smothering you with a white flag," he says with a sarcastic snarl.

"He's unlikely to be armed in a meditation centre, sir," you respond diplomatically.

"Ah. You come straight to my point. I have been asked to let you know that the government is extremely keen for Andrei Makowski to be neutralised using any means at your disposal. Do you understand what I'm saying?" His point is direct and you nod back gravely.

"The government would be delighted if Makowski could lead you to our prime target, but would like you to be aware this is not your priority tomorrow morning. I trust that I make myself clear, Sergeant?" Poe continues. This time it's apparent he wants a verbal response and you oblige him.

"Very clear," you say extinguishing the remains of your cigar.

"Excellent!" he roars. Poe is smiling again and raises himself up from his chair. He takes a white handkerchief from his trouser pocket and removes the moisture from his forehead. You feel his damp right hand clasp your shoulder as he leans in towards your ear.

"Please don't burden the official report with our chat here today. Good luck Sergeant, remember if you require any assistance contact us." Poe's hand pats you on the back before he walks off from the same direction he arrived.

The sun is momentarily hidden behind a rare cloud and you enjoy the brief decline in temperature. Having declined the waiter's offer of another drink you pay the bill. After the day's events and cryptic conversation with Poe the mind is rampant with thoughts. It would be easy to use alcohol as a palliative but you opt to wander the city in a strange catatonic state. The hours pass rapidly and you're home and asleep before dusk.

Chapter 13

The torrential rain outside wakes you ten minutes before six o'clock in the morning. Instead of attempting to fall back to sleep you lift yourself from the bed, lean back your neck and stretch. After a black coffee and half a slice of wheat toast you reach inside the top drawer of the wardrobe for your pale blue swimming shorts. They fit loosely round your waist, a sign that usually indicates good health. You slide into your navy bathing robe and create a knot around your stomach with the attached tassels.

The apartment block has a twenty five-metre length swimming pool on the ground floor. A tired looking lifeguard in his late teens is completing administrative duties on a large laptop outside the changing rooms. The young man recognises you and smiles politely before handing you a thin white towel.

It takes you forty minutes of breaststroke to swim one kilometre. The sweat pours from your shaved palate as you run on the stop in the steam room for five minutes. A cold shower shocks you awake and relieves any tension in your sore muscles. Back in your apartment you drink more coffee until refreshed enough to get dressed. A weather forecast indicates high temperatures and humidity. You put on a pair of grey slim fit trousers, navy polo shirt and sockless black loafers. The small government issued gun fits tightly into the back of your trousers and you leave your apartment before nine.

The city is busy with commuters hurriedly making their way to work. You decide to avoid the intense heat of the crammed tram and begin walking to your destination. Sunset Meditation Centre is situated on a small beach to the south of the city and you estimate it will take an hour to walk there. Swarms of automatons in sweat stained suits speed past you in a blur of motion. One obese young man in a cheap burgundy suit curses loudly as he drops his coffee on the pavement. Gradually the incessant movement of harassed government workers and office drones dissipates. In the distance you see the sun reflecting on the placid ocean.

Sunset Meditation is the largest of three buildings built directly onto the coastline. The smallest is a seemingly exclusive retirement home. Outside on beautifully constructed decking is an elderly woman being fed by a pleasant looking nurse, who smiles genially as you stroll past. Opposite this is an antique shop specialising in framed cinema posters of westerns. On the front of the remaining building is a small silver plaque, with the initials SMC. You knock on the aqua blue door and wait. It takes a few minutes before the door opens to reveal a petite red haired woman in her late forties.

"Please come in," she says quietly. The eyes are friendly and she has an attractive smile that makes one feel at ease.

"I hope you haven't been waiting very long. We aren't expecting any new clients until this evening," she asks.

"I'm not a client. I work for the government in an advisory role," you calmly reply and then hand her your relevant identity card.

"My name is Isobel, we prefer informality here at Sunset. How can I help you then Sergeant?" she continues.

"It's an extremely sensitive matter Isobel and I wish my visit to be remain confidential," you state sternly, whilst she nods back subserviently.

"The department I represent has someone experiencing acute personal problems, which I'm led to believe you could assist with. This individual is a high profile member of his Majesty's Government, who requires a degree of discretion on your part," you finish.

"I complete understand, Sergeant; we keep all files on clients confidential. After six months they are deleted from our database," she replies earnestly.

"This is excellent news, Isobel," you say before touching her shoulder with feigned relief.

"I could show you round the centre before we discuss the financial implications of staying at Sunset," she offers helpfully.

"Thank you," you reply, nodding enthusiastically. You follow her through to a brief tour of an immaculate kitchen. A plump middle-aged man in a white uniform shakes your hand firmly. The table is already set for dinner and there is an assortment of tuna and salmon sandwiches on seven separate plates.

"We start serving in fifteen minutes," claims the man you presume to be the chef.

A mounted television screen on the wall dominates the lounge. There is a carved table at the centre of the room and two large leather sofas of equal proportions. Sat on one of these is a gaunt young man in his mid-thirties. He has his unshaven face in his hands and appears to have been sobbing.

"This is Paul. He joined us yesterday evening," says Isobel and you offer the latest guest a warm handshake. The man doesn't reciprocate and his jaundiced eyes are noticeable when he raises his head. The impromptu tour continues upstairs.

"Most of our clients just require rest and perspective. The first few days prove to be the toughest. Here we are, this room is currently unoccupied," she states before opening the door of room 10. There is single bed pushed against the left hand side of the room. The minimalist décor involves an acrylic desk, foldable wooden chair and wardrobe. You glance at a rolled up foam mat in the corner.

"That's for meditating in the mornings," she points out noticing your perplexed expression. Isobel then opens the wardrobe for a brief inspection before suggesting that you the tour continue outside.

The grass outside is neatly trimmed and you notice the sprinklers at either side of the turf. Surrounding the bright green blades is immaculately polished decking. There is a silver haired man sat with his legs crossed and eyes closed. The hands are resting on his knees and his stomach is bloated as he slowly inhales breath. Underneath his body is a light blue mat, which shows the imprints from previous meditations. Behind the man dark wooden hut no higher than six feet, next to this is a used Jacuzzi with steam rises from the placid water.

"That's the steam room," your host informs you. The two of you make your way to the steps that lead onto the beach. Three figures are laid flat on the sand about a hundred metres in front.

"Are they clients?" you enquire.

"Yes, they're meditating before dinner. It's something we recommend."

"Can I meet them?" you continue. She agrees and beckons you to follow her. The largest of the clients has a book placed on his stomach, which you notice rising up and down. It is clearly a man, with broad shoulders and an extraordinarily thick neck. He is undoubtedly tall and as your proximity increases you notice how his tanned topless body. There is definition to the muscles and a thin three-inch scar below the neck. Andrei Makowski was left with this mark after coming off a bicycle in France. He still has metal screws holding together the bones in his right shoulder. Mak is now lying with his back to you in damp sand, eyes closed and unarmed.

"It's dinner time folks," Isobel shouts like a hospital matron. Mak lifts up the book that's nestling on his stomach. You watch the thick bound text sinking as he exhales. The two men on either side of your former colleague stand up and turn to Isobel like well-trained domestic animals. They then swiftly make their way to the decking steps to prepare for food. Mak sits up and stretches his back, massaging his own neck. You take a few footsteps closer and feel your heart pounding erratically.

"I didn't know you could read books Mak," you say sardonically.

Chapter 14

Andrei Makowski is staring at you with an expressionless face. The broad shoulders are carved like pieces of marble hanging over his gargantuan barrel chest. Isobel stares at you both and senses a palpable tension.

"Do you know this gentlemen, Andrei?" she states quietly to Mak. His face contorts into a broad grin and his eyes squint. You notice a small bead of sweat trickle down his forehead as he nods.

"We are old friends," he says. He holds out his hand and begins to walk towards you. You cautiously wipe your right hand of sweat so you can respond to this gesture. Before your hands meet Mak hurtles the book he is holding directly at your midriff. It rebounds painfully off your chest and you groan in pain. The knees buckle under this impact and you capitulate. He then tackles you to the floor, pinning your shoulders to the earth with his ample frame. Isobel is screaming manically.

"Gentlemen, please!" she shouts before fleeing the scene. Mak throws a small succession of heavy blows to your face, which your trapped hands are unable to cushion.

"You rotten bastard," he snarls and you feel his sweat pour onto your face. He is now paying meticulous attention to your stomach. The punches fly rapidly and you feel vomit rise through your throat. The onslaught continues as he drags you to your feet by the blood soaked polo shirt.

"It's time for a swim!" He kicks you firmly in the back and your face sinks into the damp sand.

"Did you bring any swimming shorts?" he whispers sarcastically into your ear. You stagger towards the sea feeling disorientated and barely able to stand. He grips the neck and plunges your head into the ocean. The ice-cold temperature of the sea startles you awake.

"Mak, we can make a deal!" you shout pathetically. Unfortunately, this incenses him further and he crunches his elbow down onto your back. You reach out for your back in agony and notice the petite gun still embedded in the drenched trousers. Unable to touch this weapon Makowski pushes you firmly in the chest. The aching body has little fight left and you collapse in a heap. His impressive frame is now towering over you.

"How does it feel?" Mak enquires as he takes five steps back. This provides invaluable time and rest bite from the slaughter. Pulling the gun from the drenched trousers you take aim. He begins laughing in a high-pitched shrill.

"Hands in the air please, Mak," you plead. The laughter becomes louder as he takes a step forward.

"Please, Mak. This is not what I want," you say into his unsympathetic eyes. The laughter stops but Mak makes a further two steps forward and you pull the trigger back firmly. The gunshot noise echoes along the coast and Andrei Makowski slumps back onto the beach. You keep the gun aimed on him and inspect the body. The bullet has penetrated his forehead and a small amount a blood is weeping from the wound. Mak is dead. The gun is warm and your right ear is ringing. The arm relaxes and you allow the weapon to fall from your grip. The bones ache and the nausea is overwhelming. Resting your exhausted body on the damp sand you let sleep take hold.

It's pitch black outside when your eyelids stretch open. You can feel thin sheets covering your numb body and notice the low humming noise of the air conditioning. There is a rake thin Doctor in her twenties hovering over the long bed.

"How are you sir?" she enquires.

"You tell me?" you reply sardonically. She pads out a pillow and helps you sit up.

"The body has been through quite a battering. We've administered you with several potent palliatives," she explains clinically.

"What time is it?" you ask politely.

"It's midnight, Sergeant," she informs you coldly before shining a small torch into both of your eyes. The young Doctor then examines data on her new patient's status and leaves.

It takes seconds for you to drift off to sleep and only the opening of the door, four hours later, wakes you up. In front of the bed in a red Aran knit jumper stands Poe. The Colonel is wearing denim trousers, beige sandals and appears to be holding a leather folder. He walks closer to the foot of the bed and begins clapping his hands softly.

"Congratulations on a superb operation," the face is beaming with pride. You frown back perplexed by his appearance.

"I'm permitted to wear casual clothes sometimes Sergeant," he says grasping his bizarre attire.

"Where am I, sir?" you enquire.

"A private hospital with government connections," he responds then sits on the bed, deliberately avoiding your legs.

"Did you bring any grapes, sir?" you ask dryly. He massages your right foot and smiles.

"The higher echelons are impressed Sergeant. The neutralisation of Baker and Makowski is a huge propaganda victory."

"Neutralisation?" you ask Poe mischievously but he ignores you.

"These men were symbols of an archaic ideology that has long since died. Citizens need housing and jobs not false dreams. All that remains now is William Dudek."

"The kid won't be easy to find," you reply.

"We understand that Sergeant, which is why I've been instructed to give you this," he says opening the folder. There are three photos of the kid that Poe holds up like exhibits in a court. Dudek is bearded in the final picture, which you're told is only two weeks old.

"There are a number of documents, receipts from restaurants, witness interviews and valuable leads," he states before removing a single sheet from the pile of paperwork. The document is white with 'Government Property' printed in red ink at the top.

"Please read this, Sergeant," Poe slides the paper under your eye line and you begin reading. He allows no more than a minute for you to scan the information.

"It's quite an inducement," the Colonel interrupts you, unable to contain his anticipation.

"I just have to sign this?" you ask and he nods back with assurance.

"You will own the apartment; receive a ten thousand Euro bonus and promotion to Captain. Simply sign the agreement and conclude this investigation. We rarely get second chances in this life Sergeant," he argues then removes an expensive fountain pen from his trouser pocket.

"Fifteen thousand," you reply and he grins back conspiratorially.

"I don't think that will be a problem," he places the pen in your hand and you sign accordingly.

"The Government suggests you rest here for three days. I have personally submitted the report on today's incident at Sunset Recovery. The staff there has all been briefed on how to respond to the media." Poe returns to his business like delivery.

Colonel Poe gathers all the various documentation into his leather folder. He seems keen to evacuate the scene of his sales pitch and you only have one more question.

"What if the media speak to me?" you ask as he grasps the door handle.

"They won't, Sergeant," he replies curtly and you look at him despondently.

"The Government has dealt with every eventuality. It's time to recuperate before the most challenging aspect of this assignment," he states in a reassuringly calm manner. You hear Poe exchange pleasantries with the doctor outside the room and then drift into a deep sleep.

Chapter 15

It is five days later and you're sat outside a café two minutes' walk from your apartment. On the table in front of you are three photos of William Dudek. The first is a faded black and white picture showing the kid leaving Mike Flannery's bar Osaka with Mak. The one laid next to this is a strip of passport photos of the Kid smiling with a non-descript brunette girl in her early twenties. The third picture is the most recent and depicts Dudek topless on a beach with the same brunette. His hair is almost white blonde and neatly trimmed and he's grinning through a thick auburn beard. The shoulders are still broad and defined but he's visibly gained weight. There is tension on the swimming shorts and his stomach hangs neatly over the waistband.

"Can I get you anything else, sir?" asks a slim waiter in his mid-thirties.

"I'll have another of these please," you reply raising a near empty glass of beer. He returns swiftly with beer that he places opposite the photos on a small wooden mat. Its ice cold and you take a generous gulp cooling your brow with the glass. It's a glorious day and you lean back facing the beaming sun. You still feel sore and have sporadic sharp pains in the back but fortunately no bones were broken. Poe took you for a late lunch yesterday to confirm your promotion and offer advice. After his suggestions that Mike Flannery be questioned further you nodded back politely. He seemed to be relishing his self-anointed position of mentor as he tore into his absurdly well-done steak.

Mike would not only be uncooperative now but possibly ill informed. He would never forgive what had happened to Mak and the Kid's visits to Osaka so rare that he wouldn't know anything. The real lead was this young woman who'd shared a photo booth with William Dudek.

The woman can't be more than twenty-five years old. She has no signs of wrinkles under the eyes and the lips are still generous despite the cigarette in the final picture. Her dark brown hair is fashionable short with a small streak of purple die in the fringe. She is neither particularly striking nor unattractive, apart from noticeable piercing grey blue eyes. These eyes and this fleck of dyed hair will be the key to locating her and indeed the Kid.

Dudek has only ever seen one type of woman. She's young, idealistic and understands the kid. You remember fondly how he fell for a nineteen-year-old lap dancer fresh off the boat from France saying,

"She completely gets me. I've never felt this way," he spouted like a lovelorn puppy. There is only one person who will be able to help you track her down, and he's ironically now employed in the government ranks. You sink the rest of your beer; order a plastic container of espresso coffee and walk to the nearest tram stop. Most government departments are situated in the city centre near the vast shopping centres and are only five stops away.

It's nearly one when you arrive in the city centre. There are hundreds of young students clasping shopping bags containing their latest purchases. The different youth subcultures are an amalgamation of all the divergent styles from the last hundred years. There is a group of young men and women outside the station indicative of this look. The young women have tight-skinned linen tops of various colours matched with slim black denim trousers and sockless labour boots. Their male counterparts are wearing white and pink oxford collar shirts, paint on chinos and sockless loafers. Both sexes are smoking self-consciously in the manner of new wave film actor and one young man has a beautifully crafted fedora perched on his head.

The Department of Counter Domestic Terror is the smallest and most discreet of the government buildings. It's a five-minute walk from the station steps where you dropped the empty espresso flask into a nearby bin. Sat behind a desk in a tight grey dress is a woman approaching forty. She stands up revealing a thick navy coloured belt.

"I have an appointment with your scenario analyst," you say handing her a new identity card.

"Colonel Poe informed us of this visit late yesterday. Please walk this way, Captain," her reminder of this promotion jars slightly but you dutifully follow her down a long corridor. All the wooden doors are closed and numbered in small italic font. When you reach number twenty-two she gives a solicitous smile and gestures to enter.

"Thanks," you reply and open the door into a brightly lit office and a well-furnished and attractive room. The floor is sanded down wood so familiar with government décor. There are well-framed Turner replicas on the walls and a burgundy coloured rug lies stylishly over the wooden panels. In the corner of the room is a tall slim lampshade the same colour as the rug. The furniture consists of a beautifully polished glass table with the sunlight from the opened window gleaming off the surface. Two deep burgundy leather chairs perched in front of this desk have grey cushions. Sat behind the desk in a slightly larger version of these chairs is your host.

"Please take a seat, Captain," he offers cheerfully. He's a slim but athletically built young man in his mid-thirties and his thinning hair hidden well by a short cut. He stands up and pours himself a piping hot drink into a china mug with no handle.

"Tea?" he enquires and you accept. He has slim khaki trousers on, a checked pink shirt and navy tie with pink coloured flecks in the fabric pattern. The young man takes a seat and wiggles his toes inside the shiny black loafers on his feet. You sip the tea, which is beautifully sweet and refreshing.

"Any luck with my request?" you ask trying to avoid any banal chatter.

"Yes I'll get the file I've compiled," he states obligingly and limps towards a pine table with documents neatly piled up.

"Please forgive me Captain but this wound has a mind of its own on occasion," he says patting his right knee lightly and continues,

"I wasn't always sat behind this desk wearing loud shirts. A hair-raising assignment in the east ten years ago," he speaks elegantly and even with the limp carries an air of dignity.

"A bullet shattered the kneecap completely. Now let's look at the file." He sits back down and places the document in front of you. It is a transparent plastic folder designed that resembles an envelope. On the front is a thin tag with the words 'Urgent request for Colonel Poe: Compiled by Major Jacob Brummell' printed in bold ink. Major Brummell then removes all pictures and printed documents you requested via Poe. He places an enlarged photo of the woman seen leaving Osaka with the kid. It seems like a graduation picture from a few years hence and her hair is longer than the previous snapshot.

"Her name is Ruth Coleridge; she's twenty-six years old and was a fairly extreme radical when studying a Graphic and Fashion design degree at the City University. Good background with both parents teaching in the same school. Miss Coleridge has three arrests but nothing serious. These have focused themes like pro-migration marches and vandalism, which has usually involved advertising companies. The minor offences won't exist on too many systems. The only link to any of these activities is they were all organised by the same person, John Werther. Do you know this man?" he asks after a concise summary of the suspect. After nodding affirmatively you ask about the kid and he answers promptly.

"Mr Dudek believes himself to be a noble savage even if he doesn't fully understand what this means."

Chapter 16

Major Jacob Brummel leans back massaging his left cheek with the right palm. He removes a picture of the kid and presses his index finger onto Dudek's three-inch scar.

"I believe that Mr Dudek has constructed his own perception of himself through how others view him. A young individual like Dudek is susceptible to father figures and pseudo intellectuals like Werther," he explains concisely.

"Do you think that this Ruth Coleridge has introduced them?" you politely interrupt.

"Exactly," he replies enthusiastically. The Major then slides out a colour photo of John Werther. It's the prison photo taken on his arrest seven months ago. Werther's flaxen hair is auburn and silver at the temples. The brown eyes seem fixated on the photographer and are squinting, which highlights the wrinkles stretching across his face. His thin lips are smirking ironically and the top three buttons of his red shirt are open.

"Dudek has become more active since his involvement with this man. Werther has encouraged a latent belief that he is a 'noble savage' through his connection to Miss Coleridge. If you can find her Captain you find the Kid," he states empathically.

"A noble savage?" you politely ask.

"Dudek was originally attracted to the cause for pure hedonistic reasons and this is why his criminal activity had been so sporadic. The reason he's a threat to the government now, is because Werther has helped politicise these actions," he explain with fervour before continuing.

"Werther has no doubt legitimatised the Kid's errant behaviour as individual defiance against an unjust society and therefore…"

"Therefore his criminal behaviour will increase in both grandeur and activity because he now believes he's justified," you interrupt the young officer.

Major Jacob Brummell and you sit quietly for a moment aware of the magnitude of his conclusion. If William Dudek isn't apprehended with haste then his violent conduct will begin to endanger the public not just the government.

"Well thanks for this information, sir," you say before standing up and gathering all documents into the folder.

"Good luck, Captain," he replies and holds out his hand, which you shake firmly in gratitude. It takes only a few minutes to leave the Department of Counter Domestic Terror building and you're hungry. There is a modest restaurant down a small alley, which serves decent food.

The restaurant is called Wuxi and caters for the increasing number of people who dine alone. There are four wooden tables outside on the pavement. You take a seat at one still in the sunlight and order a medium rare steak with baby potatoes. The female waitress brings you a pot of tea while you wait and pour slowly. As the steam rises from the thick-based mug you open up the folder compiled by Brummell. You take a large gulp of tea and spread all the files relating to John Werther on the oak coloured table.

John Werther was born over fifty years ago in one of the Western Isles of Scotland that have been inhabitable for nearly three decades. His ancestors had been weavers in a successful mill there for generations. Unfortunately, the demand for the materials they produced and increased temperatures rendered all companies like this obsolete. Despite this he received a private education on the outskirts of the nation's capital before attending the exclusive Architecture and Design College based not far from the hospital Poe visited you in.

There was a huge demand for architects as the government realised the potential impact of environmental change on city planning. Werther was young, ambitious and favoured the minimalist style of the Far East. This was precisely what the multitude of politicians sought, simple cost effective and easy to construct. The marketing companies labelled these buildings 'Zen Flats', which gave them a glamorous image that was undeserving. Unqualified labourers feebly constructed these apartments and the flats that were completed became cramped havens for petty crime and squalor. You remember during your days with the cause being assigned to destroy a barely built one with Mak. It capitulated so quickly that you were both nearly buried by the rubble.

John Werther became a wealthy and successful man. The marketing departments duly manipulated him. He agreed to give orchestrated interviews to the media and was the public image for the 'Zen Flats'. This all changed eight years ago when one of the coastal apartment blocks collapsed injuring seventy eight people and killing thirty two. Werther hadn't even designed the flats but the ensuing crisis needed a scapegoat and he was thrown to the media.

The government got him a relatively well-paid job lecturing post at the college he'd attended as a student. Werther's appetites for alcohol and the more impressionable female students in his class did not go unnoticed. When he became an unlikely campus activist against the government, the cumulative effect of this lost him his job.

Other educational institutes employed him. As his teaching positions and pay became less lucrative though, his political activity became more acute. He began organising terror attacks on government buildings, some of which he'd designed. Then six months ago he planned and executed the destruction of the newly built Department for Economic Welfare. The attack took place early in the morning, just after six o'clock. Seven young cleaners were killed and John Werther was now a dangerous murdered wanted by the government. It didn't surprise you how quickly he was apprehended but the remorseless statement he gave to the media upon his arrest took you aback.

The steak tastes delicious and you chew slowly savouring every bite. The baby potatoes are lavished in thick butter and you finish the meal quickly. The waitress deserves a generous tip and you leave one before beginning the walk to your apartment. It is late evening now, but still extremely close and before arriving home conclude that a swim will clear the mind.

When you slump into your apartment chair you notice how exhausted the body and mind have become. Before this lethargy can take hold you raise yourself up and quickly assemble everything you need for a swim. You don't recognise the innocent face of the female lifeguard who you assume is new. She is sat in an uncomfortable plastic chair studiously observing the three swimmers already in the pool. She smiles as you remove your robe and you smile back before submerging into the water.

You swim breaststroke without rest for about an hour and pull yourself out having failed to count a single length. There is a recently opened steam room that you sit in for ten minutes with your head leaning forward. Small sweat particles drip from your forehead, whilst you contemplate the remaining obstacles of the assignment. There is rest bite from the gallivanting thoughts racing through your mind in a cold shower adjacent the steam room.

It's dark in the flat now and you boil some milk and pour the contents into a mug. The piping hot liquid trickles down the throat and insulates your stomach. Another challenging day awaits and it will require mental guile and physical agility to cross exam John Werther. He is situated in a high-level security prison about eight tram stops away. It seems a harsh place to incarcerate for their first term of sentence but Werther is again being used as a scapegoat. This time to show the speedy and efficient work of the government's state paid Police. Fortunately the vilified John Werther will have his own cell and be in constant isolation. However, this doesn't mean he will be pleased to see you.

Chapter 17

It's early when you wake, still pitch black outside and just gone five in the morning. The humidity is almost unbearable and when you lean back into the pillow you're submerged in damp sweat. Small heavy pains of rain hammering at the apartment windows convince you that any further sleep will be impossible. The arms ache from swimming and your mood is low. You rise up from bed and perform some gentle stretches to invigorate your defunct bones. After one strong black coffee your mind shakes off any remaining slumber and you take a second coffee to the window and stare out.

At the nearby tram stop there are already three commuters seeking protection from the rain. The shelter is transparent and a light makes it easy to identify them. A large white haired lady in the government cleaner's uniform is sat clasping what looks like a hot drink. On a seat next to her is a young man in his late teens wearing slim black jeans. His white linen jacket is sodden and he keeps yawning, perhaps due to the previous evening's festivities. The final commuter is a well-dressed man in his forties. He keeps straightening his tie in the reflection of the shelter and fidgeting with his watch.

After an ice cold shower and shave you reason that it's still too early for breakfast and have a final coffee and change. Despite the intense heat you opt for formal dress and put on a three-piece beige linen suit. A navy woollen tie fits smoothly under the collar of your pink shirt. The tan brown loafers have never been worn and they pinch on the toes. However, they have plastic soles with grips ideal for inclement weather. You put on a slim navy raincoat, check the pockets for identity cards and put on your brown wide rimmed fedora. It takes just a few minutes before your standing where the three commuters stood moments earlier.

On the platform is a government-funded vending device that's newly installed. You insert three Euros and remove a Health Department approved 'Niacin Bar' from the wrapping. It's coated in a thin layer of low fat chocolate, which is the only thing that makes it edible. There is a low humming sound in the distance signifying the arrival of a tram. The tram doors slide open and you take a seat removing your damp fedora. You move your neck from left to right to reduce any soreness remaining after you slept awkwardly listening to vinyl records. A female cleaner sat opposite observes you with a perplexed expression. You smile back apologetically then place the fedora over the eyelids like a visor.

The carriages grind to a halt a total of seven times before you rise from an uncomfortable seat and re-adjust the navy tie using the trams convex mirror. You notice you've cut your chin shaving and you rub the dry blood away using an index finger. It is still early morning when you step off the tram into the rain. The time is irrelevant because all high-level detention centres remain accessible twenty-four hours of the day. There are no shops, cafes or restaurants within the vicinity of the prison. The government workers are expected to dine on site or bring pre-prepared food to work.

No other passengers have terminated their journey at this stop and you make a solitary walk to the grey building on the other side of the tracks. The fourth of six high-level security prisons is a grotesque building with three storeys. There is a discreet sign next to the entrance that states 'Maximum Security: No Un-authorised Visitors' in thick red print on a white background. You press the button next to a minute microphone and announce your arrival. The door slides open as you remove the credentials from your pocket.

In the centre of the prison entrance hall are two middle-aged women sat upright behind an oak desk. Both women are wearing the same distinct uniform of bale blue shirts, long black skirts and sensible shoes. The thinner of the women is sat on the left with a portable electronic identity screen. She has her white hair tied back into a tight bob, whilst her red haired co-worker is typing diligently into her government laptop. It's contraband for female prison workers to wear make-up and both these women adhere to this draconian ideal.

"Can I help you, sir?" the larger of the two ladies enquires looking up from her laptop. You don't reply and hand her the relevant documentation required for your visit. She examines these intensely then turns to her colleague and nods sternly.

"Please," the white haired lady states passing you the electronic tablet. There are five authorised appointments for today and you press on screen next to your initials and government rank.

"Thank you, Captain," she replies cheerfully retrieving her identity screen.

"Please take a seat. Sergeant Flint has been notified of your arrival," she says then gestures to the comfortable leather seats close to her desk. You nod back silently and lean back into the nearest chair.

It takes Sergeant Flint under ten minutes to join you in the entrance hall. He's well over six foot tall and has an impressive figure. His blonde hair is shaved short and has tanned skin. The thick neck rests neatly on huge chiselled shoulders and toned arms and the pale blue shirt looks painted on.

"I apologise for an undue waiting, sir." He hands out his right hand and offers you a firm handshake.

"Not a problem, Sergeant," you reply politely.

"The prisoner has been moved to an interrogation room and is waiting for us there. Please follow me sir," he states efficiently. It's the first time a Sergeant has dealt with you so subserviently and it feels surreal and unwanted. You follow him dutifully and attempt to engage in conversation.

"How many prisoners are staying here, Sergeant?" you ask professionally.

"We currently have nine inmates and the facilities to incarcerate a further three if necessary. These are extremely dangerous men and an acute threat to His Majesty's Government sir."

You follow him into a lift, which takes you both down to the lower ground floor. When the lift doors open you notice how the corridor is dimly lit and there are only two doors. The Sergeant stands outside one of them brandishing a door key, which he's removed from his shirt pocket.

"The prisoner will be seated behind a small transparent desk wearing a white t-shirt, white trousers and beige slip on shoes. Please do not antagonise this man Sir," he warns you.

"Why?" you enquire.

"He is a dangerous murderer who will never be released from this institute," he continues.

"I thought he was an architect?" you ask sarcastically because this officious young man is beginning to annoy you. He stands unresponsive glaring hypnotically ahead and you speak to avoid any delay.

"Can we go in now, Sergeant?" you ask him. He opens the door pushing it ajar before leaning into your left ear.

"I will be in the room during the entire interview sir," he whispers.

The room is brightly lit by four bulbs imbedded into the ceiling and has one table in the middle of the room. It's indeed transparent and the prisoner is dressed entirely in white. You take a seat in the steel fold out chair on the other side of the table. Sergeant Flint is leaning on the wall behind your right shoulder and has crossed his arms to accentuate the bicep muscles. After taking a seat you slide the folder Brummell compiled closer to the prisoner. This causes Flint to clear his throat loudly but you continue,

"How are you, Mr Werther?"

Chapter 18

John Werther looks different to the media reports, photos and interviews you've seen. His visibly has lost weight with the generous chins and round cheeks replaced by the gaunt haunted visage observing you now. The ruddy complexion is still there, remnants of sustained alcohol abuse. Werther's thick auburn hair has been shaved short and he's grown an unflattering military style moustache. The shoulders are broad and the physique, like many prisoners, is trim and defined.

"Answer the Captain's question!" barks Sergeant Flint.

"Who are you?" asks Werther maintaining a blank expression.

"I'm a government official," you reply diplomatically. He smiles back knowingly then looks up at Flint and nods disapprovingly.

"A messenger boy," he says condescendingly without making eye contact with either of you before continuing,

"Now I've established what you are I'd like to know what you want," his brown eyes fixed on the young Sergeant. Werther has a repellent misplaced arrogance and talks like all pseudo intellectuals. He's performing to an audience that no longer exists and you feel compelled to ask Flint to leave the room.

"I realise you're a very busy man Mr Werther and you can return to staring at the cell walls shortly," you say glaring back at him with intent. He spends the next minute looking at the wall while his face turns red.

"You're a real charmer aren't you, Captain?" he eventually replies calming himself down using deep breathing.

"We'd like your opinion on an investigation being carried out."

"What do I get out of this exchange of ideas?" He responds curtly and winks at Flint who looks perplexed by proceedings.

"Nothing. I don't give a shit if you help me or not," you snap back aggressively and then outline the predicament Werther finds himself.

"Mr Werther you're a high profile convicted murderer who will spend the rest of his life here. People like yourself are in no position to bargain with anyone," you explain coldly. He looks crestfallen and buries his head into both hands. After rubbing his temples for a few moments he sits up erect and straightens his t-shirt. He then holds out his right hand as if expecting a gift.

"Give me the file," he says quietly and you place the folder in his hand. Flint watches pensively whilst Werther removes all the relevant photos and documents.

"Handsome man," he says holding up the photo of himself from seven months ago. Werther looks startled when examining the next photo and seems momentarily paralysed. This is replaced by an uproarious laugh as he slams both hands on the transparent desk.

"The prisoner will calm down!" shouts Flint as an objective fact rather than a request.

"Forgive me Sergeant but I know these people," he says pointing at the photo of the kid and Ruth leaving Mike's bar. He holds up the photo for you to see and grins conspiratorially.

"You didn't say you were hunting wild animals Captain," John Werther says dryly.

"Do you know where he is?" you ask him with an air of desperation.

"Why does everyone imagine I know the whereabouts of William Dudek? It was the first thing those incompetent cretins asked when I was arrested," he replies vacantly before rubbing his head in feigned confusion. You grasp the photo and turn it round to face him.

"Where is Ruth Coleridge?" you shout pressing your finger onto her face.

"You're not as stupid as you look Captain. That's your plan isn't it? Find Ruth and you'll find the Kid?" he enquires earnestly.

"Where is Ruth Coleridge?" you repeat rapidly losing your temper.

"You'll get nothing off me on Ruth you moron!" he responds folding his arms and turning his head to the wall. This incenses you and leaping from the chair you grab the front of his t-shirt and strike him firmly in the face twice.

"Listen you pretentiously prick I'm not leaving here until you tell me everything I'd like to know," you're still seething with anger and genuine loathing. You turn back and see a stationary Sergeant Flint with his back turned facing the wall. You smile and raise your fist again, which Werther notices in the corner of his eye.

"Okay, Captain! I'll cooperate!" Werther whimpers and you release your grip watching him slump into his chair. Flint turns round with an ironic smile and you nod back.

"I met Ruth at the City College when she was studying a Fashion degree. There was an organised protest against government tax increases. She was so intelligent, erudite and passionate," he explained with an air of nostalgia.

"Do like passionate young girls Werther?" you interrupt sarcastically and watch with pleasure as Flint grins.

"It wasn't like that Captain. Ruth wouldn't consort in a sordid campus romance with a lecturer. I was her mentor and nothing else!" he barks raising his voice at the end.

"She would visit my office every day after lectures to discuss numerous topics. We'd drink tea and exchange ideas for hours. Ruth had a genuine desire for constructive and peaceful social change. It was me who advocated violence in extreme circumstances and not her," he says solemnly.

"What happened?" you ask.

"William Dudek happened?" he replies with an air of regret.

"When did they meet?"

"I don't know the exact circumstances but it was about a year ago. She'd started to become involved in more extreme government protests and I believe was even arrested a handful of times. Then about a month before my unfortunate fall from grace Ruth visited my office with an unusual young man. I'd been accused of drunken incompetence by the college and assumed she was there to offer support," he states dabbing down the blood from his face.

"What did she want?" you enquire.

"She was there to introduce Mr Dudek as a key figure in the cause against government exploitation. He was polite and softly spoken candidly explaining his political beliefs. There was an undoubted charisma about this young man with the thin scar on his face. There was a savagery to his character that if curbed could prove invaluable. They came to my office a further three times. With each visit I attempted to introduce William to the more subtle intricacies of a potential revolution."

"How did he respond?" you ask.

"He seemed intrigued with my suggestion that he had potential as a leader. I encouraged him to read some of the literature that I'd passed onto Ruth. In each discussion he would come with pre-prepared questions on the books he'd read," he explains proudly.

"Then what happened?" you ask impatiently.

"I was politely asked to vacate the college campus and cordially invited here," he replies looking up at the ceiling.

"Where is Ruth Coleridge?" you ask Werther aware of the question's magnitude. John Werther is a tragic figure sat slumped in a t-shirt decorated in his own blood and remains silent for nearly a minute. He then straightens his back into a position of dignity and his brown eyes stare at you.

"Every evening at seven o'clock she goes to a bar near the city college to meet friends. It's called Breath," his voice is clear and you smile at him in gratitude before leaving.

Chapter 19

Outside the detention centre is an extravagantly dressed Colonel Poe dabbing sweat beads from his forehead. He's wearing a jet-black linen suit over a garish yellow waistcoat. On his feet are brown loafers and Poe is waving aloft a cane to get your attention. Considering the ill-advised shoes and waistcoat this isn't necessary. You wave back in acknowledgement and walk towards him.

"Hello, sir," you say shaking his hand.

"Have you had a productive morning, Captain?" he responds business-like.

"I think so, sir. Mr Werther was most cooperative and has provided us with an invaluable lead," you explain optimistically.

"I've never doubted your powers of persuasion," he says caressing Werther's dried blood on your waistcoat.

"He's a rather tragic figure now, sir," you reply softly moving his hand from your garment.

"Do you know where to find Ruth Coleridge?" he asks you, wasting no time.

"I'm hopeful of locating her this evening at a student bar near the city college," you state omitting the name of the bar. He rubs his stomach, which is bulging through the jacket material and feigns a look of contemplation.

"Will you be apprehending this young lady?" he enquires scratching the back of his neck.

"I don't think that will be necessary sir. The primary objective remains identifying the location of William Dudek and I believe she is the key to this," you reply calmly.

"This is exhilarating news Captain but we must proceed with care. As this assignment approaches a conclusion a number of things need to be considered," he tells you pointing in the air.

"What do you mean?" you ask in genuine confusion.

"As I have stated on previous encounters the higher echelons of the government have been extremely pleased with your thoroughness. I don't think it will come as a surprise that someone with your shadowy past wasn't everyone's first choice," he explains and you nod back encouraging him to continue.

"When Mr Dudek is finally neutralised we will enter the most delicate part of this operation. William Dudek is an exceptionally charismatic personality, which makes him such a dangerous individual. He is already popular amongst the city's migrant population and the last thing the government desires is another martyr to the cause."

"What do they want me to do?" you ask.

"They want you to make it easier for the government's various marketing and media departments. Their job will be to present Dudek as a dangerous moral vacuum intent on destroying the moral fabric of our society. This would be made incredible difficult if any harm came to an innocent twenty-six year old fashion graduate," he continues.

"Innocent?" you ask aghast at the suggestion.

"We both know the reality of the situation but I trust we both understand whose side we are on. It is the government that pays for your apartment, the furniture and those stylish clothes you are so fond of. Do you understand, Captain?" he asks earnestly.

"I understand," you reply coldly.

"Excellent. I'm going to need the name of this bar too," he enquires.

"It's called Breath. It's a five-minute walk from the city college tram stop. I was going to visit there this evening about seven o'clock. If Ruth Coleridge is there I had intended to follow her and hopefully locate the kid," you say summarising your plan.

"That remains an exceptionally good idea. However it has been decided that my colleagues and I will accompany you. This way we can avoid any potential pitfalls at this late stage," he states before tapping you softly on the chest with the end of his cane.

It is five hours later and you are speeding along the tramlines to the city college tram stop. Poe gave you ample time to change at your apartment whilst he notified his subordinates. The weather had changed rapidly into a rare blustery day and you exchanged the suit for khaki trousers, red polo shirt and your black windbreaker jacket. Poe was waiting outside the apartment block for you with his two colleagues. They were both dressed in long black raincoats stood ominously on both sides of the Colonel.

The first of these associates is standing next to you on the tram and was introduced by Poe as Mr Deed. He's just over six feet in height and has shortly cropped red hair and a neatly trimmed beard in the same colour. The frame is slight but you can tell from the steel in the blue eyes that he's a dangerous man. You notice a gun slid down his charcoal grey trousers when he adjusts the long overcoat. The other man is undoubtedly armed too and you can only speculate whether Poe has a gun. The second man is smaller in height but has a robust athletic frame that stretches the fabric of his coat. He introduced himself as Mr Bradshaw and you noticed a scar on his chin running through his black stubble.

"How many more stops?" asks Mr Bradshaw.

"Two," replies the stoic Deed before you can respond. It's the first time he's spoken and you note the deep monotonous tone.

The tram is half-full but all four of you have remained standing. Most people on the tram are commuters journeying home apart from a handful of noisy students who seem taken by the black overcoats being worn by Deed and Bradshaw. Poe raises his eyebrows to garner your attention and walks towards you.

"We will get ourselves a table in the bar and order drinks," he whispers.

"What about them?" you ask looking at Poe's associates.

"Mr Deed and Mr Bradshaw will wait outside."

"They're not exactly conspicuous are they?" you reply.

"They're experienced professionals, Captain," he assures you.

It takes only a few minutes before you arrive at the relevant stop. There are very few lights still on in the main college building and the majority of students and lecturers will already be frequented the nearby bars.

"It's this way," you say to the three men and they follow accordingly. There is a young man in his late teens vomiting in an alley whilst his on looking girlfriend sways her head in disappointment. You smile and walk past noticing the sign for Breath in the distance. The time is five minutes to seven when you arrive at your destination and the four of you huddle together to discuss further action.

"We'll be sitting here, sir," Deed tells Poe pointing at one of two small outside tables. The Colonel doesn't reply and ushers you to escort him into the bar. It's extremely busy with a substantial queue at the bar and you both take at seat by a table at the back.

There are two waiters working at Breath and both are young men in their early twenties. The one closest to you is neglecting other customers in favour of talking to a group of friends who keep cajoling him and fiddling with his apron ties. Poe seems aggravated by this negligence and clicks his fingers at the busier of the two waiters.

"Excuse me, young man," he says patronising the youngster by clicking his fingers. This indiscreet behaviour and the fact Poe is still wearing the loud yellow waistcoat leaves you mildly astonished.

"Perhaps we should just sit quietly, sir," you suggest diplomatically to your superior.

"Well quite," he says suddenly aware of the idiocy of his actions. The room is well lit and there are the usual array of cinema posters and nostalgic pictures of sports heroes framed on the walls. The two glasses of whiskey are left on your table and you enjoy sipping it slowly, ignoring Poe for a few moments. As you cradle your glass a young woman with a coloured fleck of hair enters the bar.

Chapter 20

She's about five foot seven with a petite figure and far more attractive than her photograph. Ruth Coleridge is made up with bright red lipstick coated on her sensual lips. She has a large pale blue shirt, which Ruth has turned into a dress by tightly wrapping a black belt round her waist. A tall young man accompanies her with long floppy hair over the eyes. It's bleached white blonde with about an inch of black hair growing through the roots. He's extremely thin and has pale skin accentuated by his peroxide hair. The black denim trousers hang from a waistline no more than twenty-eight inches wide and there are wooden beads hanging over his plain white t-shirt.

"It's her?" Poe asks too loudly.

"Definitely, sir," you say sipping from your glass and looking in the opposite direction to Ruth Coleridge.

You observe as she spends ten minutes walking round the room kissing both male and females on both cheeks in the European manner before taking a seat at the bar. Her companion chats animatedly with the bar staff then hands her a bottle of beer.

Ruth Coleridge dominates the conversation between herself and the rake thin young man sipping on his beer. His legs are crossed revealing black leather boots with three-inch heels. Miss Coleridge gestures a lot with her hands, pointing to emphasise a point and throwing her head back in sporadic laughter.

They order two more rounds of beer as you continue glancing over every few minutes. You order another whiskey whilst Poe stares blankly at his first.

"What time is it?" Poe asks impatiently.

"It's eight o'clock sir," you reply sensing his frustration. He shuffles in his chair and turns round staring at her.

"Do you think we should make ourselves known?" he enquires.

"We need to be patient and wait for her to leave. This is the only way we can locate Dudek and deal with her in the sensitive way you suggested," you explain reminding him of his sage advice.

It's fifteen minutes past eight and you notice Ruth rise from her chair. She hugs her friend goodbye and kisses him on his pale right cheek. Ruth Coleridge then checks the contents of her purse and walks to the bar exit. Poe grips the armrests on his chair and looks at you excitedly.

"Patience, sir," you say calmly.

When she leaves the bar you stand up leaving a twenty-Euro note under the empty whiskey glass. Poe follows your lead and you head out onto the street. Outside Deed and Bradshaw stand stiffly on the opposite side of the road waiting for instruction from their Colonel. Miss Coleridge is now twenty metres down the road heading to the main college building. The four of you pursue her to the tram stop where she's leaning against the shelter brushing her hands through her short hair.

The tram carriage is sparsely populated with the only occupants, an elderly couple and a bearded man stooped forward asleep. Coleridge glances at Poe's assistants with suspicion and takes a seat at the back of the carriage facing the driver. At each stop the tram halts with no passengers boarding. The elderly couple step off five stops in and Poe leans in over your shoulder.

"Where is she going?" he whispers but you don't reply. The last station on this route was the epicentre of the cities coal mining industry. Unfortunately, the government closed these sites down decades ago and replaced the flat caps and industry with capsule hotels and solar energy. The only reason a stop exists there is because a museum dedicated to mining was recently re-opened.

At the second to last stop Ruth stands up and gently wakes up the bearded gentleman seated opposite Bradshaw and Deed. He rubs his bleary eyes and staggers onto the platform mumbling incoherently. She now observes all four of the suspicious men in her carriage including you. Poe smiles at her genially, which only increases her nervousness. She stands by the exit doors as the tram begins to slow down for the stop now called 'Industrial

88

Museum.' You see Deed unwisely step close to Ruth hovering over her shoulder as the vehicle comes to a halt.

The electronic doors slide open and Ruth Coleridge clasps her hands together before hammering her right elbow into Deed's stomach. The surprise of this blow causes him to hunch over and he groans in agony. She sprints off down the platform, straight past the closed museum into the dark of the abandoned mine. You push the incompetent Deed aside and run after her into the night air.

"Captain!" yells a despondent Colonel Poe, whilst Bradshaw pulls Deed to his feet.

You can just about see Coleridge in the distance and you wipe tears from your eyes caused by running into the wind.

"Ruth!" you shout vainly and notice a luminous light about one hundred metres ahead. It's a large fire and you observe the silhouettes of two figures dispersing from the flames. About fifty metres from the fire you take refuge behind a large pile of abandoned coal listening to rapid footsteps around you.

"I thought you wore suits these days!" a man bellows in your direction. It's the unmistakable voice of William Dudek.

"It's this bloody weather kid!" you shout back.

"I heard about Mak and Pete!" he continues bellowing.

"I'm sorry kid!" you reply mournfully before you hear a loud explosion. A bullet ricochets off a lump of coal above your head and you throw your body onto the cold concrete below. There are footsteps running behind and you pull the gun from your trousers.

"Captain!" shouts the sweat ridden Mr Bradshaw but before you can force him to the ground there is another gunshot. The bullet hits Bradshaw like a travelling brick and he hits the floor. You crawl towards him to identify where he's been hit and see bleeding on his left shoulder.

"You'll be fine just stay here," you whisper to the fortunate Bradshaw. You can hear the kid's high-pitched laughter just metres away.

"How's your new friend?" the kid says and then continues cackling incessantly. You rip off part of Bradshaw's raincoat and wrap it tightly round the injured shoulder.

"This ends one way, kid!" you shout over the lumps of coal.

Behind you are the footsteps of two men who you're relieved to see are Colonel Poe and a crest fallen Mr Deed. Poe crouches down next to you awkwardly and you grin wryly as the fabric on his suit stretches. Deed attends to his comrade quietly and assures Bradshaw it's a minor injury.

"Where's Dudek?" Poe asks urgently and another bullet cascades into the coal. You point to the direction of the gunfire.

"He's about fifty metres in that direction," you whisper quietly.

"What do you intend to do, Captain?" Poe replies shivering with fear.

"He has the advantage from his position and we can assume the kid knows this area inside out," you say trying to calm your own nerves rather than concern yourself with the Colonel's increasingly erratic behaviour. Poe drags himself to his feet and bows his head slightly.

"Where are you going, sir?" you ask.

"This situation is developing out of our control and I need to alert the government who can provide extra support," he replies nervously.

"What?" you bark back aggressively listening to the persistent laughter of the kid in the background. Unfortunately, your panic-stricken superior has made up his mind and waddles off into the darkness. The kid now has you trapped behind a pile of coal with an injured man and an incompetent government automaton.

Chapter 21

You notice that your left hand is now shaking severely and you clench your fist firmly in an attempt to remedy the problem. In the right hand you feel the coldness of your unfired government issued firearm. Deed recklessly raises his head over the top of the lumps of coal and you pull him down.

"I can see him, sir," he says with misplaced optimism.

"It's pitch black, Deed," you respond quite reasonably and try to slow your racing thoughts with slow deep breaths.

"He's probably short of ammunition and is wondering why we don't attack his position. There hasn't been any gunfire for a few minutes now."

"We wait," you state with finality. However, Mr Deed is utterly convinced he can apprehend William Dudek singlehandedly. Despite his failed attempt to intimidate Miss Coleridge on the tram he jolts up and begins running towards a faded yellow skip. You don't shout for him to return and you're impressed when he dives successfully behind his target. He raises his thumb at you and you return the gesture relieved he's still alive.

"William Dudek, we are government agents sent here to bring you to justice," Deed shouts in his deep monotonous voice. The kid responds by peppering the skip with a barrage of bullets in quick succession. You sigh at the predictability of Deed's rant and continue to think of alternative approaches to this daunting situation.

"If you present yourself to us in a peaceful manner you will be dealt with leniently," Deed continues before the kid fires at the feet, which are dangling just outside of the skip. Mr Deed retracts his feet in and offers a hollowed final warning.

"You were warned, Mr Dudek," he says and you wait in anticipation. Then you listen to a short succession of footsteps followed by a deafening gun blast. You can hear Deed's body fall to the ground but this time there is no groaning and instead there is a deathly silence.

"It's just us now," shouts the kid and you can feel the heart pounding against your chest and beads of sweat pour from the forehead. The laughter has stopped and Dudek sounds more serious and earnest.

"Where's Ruth, kid?" you shout back across the desolate land.

"Ruth's right here by my side and she's staying here," he snaps back aggressively.

"She'll be a lot safer if you release her," you plead.

"Safer! She's here because she wants to be you bastard," the kid replies snarling at the end of the sentence. You clench your left fist repeatedly to dissipate your increasing anxiety.

"Why did you do it?" the kid enquires with an air of melancholia. You'd like to tell him that you were forced and it was the only way to protect family members. Perhaps Dudek would sympathise if you explained the threat of torture or a life spent in a detention centre. He'd certainly empathise if you explained how you'd fallen in love. Unfortunately none of that is true and you know that the abiding reasons you still work for the government. Firstly you want to stay alive and grow old and secondly they pay you. These are certainly not romantic explanations of your behaviour and definitely reasons one as young as the kid couldn't fathom.

"You get older kid," you reply pathetically and wince at this response.

"What's your plan smartarse?" the kid demands realistically and you continue wracking your brain for options.

"The two clowns you brought with you are and dead and I saw that cowardly fat bastard do a runner," Dudek carries on his torrent of abuse and its only small comfort that he has miscalculated Bradshaw's demise.

"What's you plan, sir?" gasps a semi-conscious Bradshaw. If you run into the pitch black the kid will shoot you down in seconds, which isn't a viable idea. To out flank Dudek by slowly stepping quietly around his left is unrealistic. The kid will hear you and this would needlessly endanger Ruth Coleridge. Unfortunately, you're also aware that there will never be another opportunity to conclude this vile assignment. If the mission could miraculously finish this evening, they might leave you alone. You could blissfully return to the mundane duties of observations and paperwork. Poe had even hinted at a further promotion and pay increase.

"Are you going to show yourself?" the kid seems perplexed by your silence and you note that Bradshaw has passed out. You decide to take action and no matter how reckless this will be you need to disrupt the kid's thought process and panic him. The gun slides neatly between two lumps of coal nestled on the pile and you can see the dark outline of Dudek's figure. You stand erect and place your eyes over the sights and aim the gun just below his feet. When you pull the trigger, there is a deafening noise in your left ear and the area is briefly lit up. The kid roars out in agony and you see him stumble to the floor.

"You sneaky bastard!" he screams, dragging himself backwards clasping his left thigh. Before he disappears into the darkness he fires randomly towards the coal but misses and dirt from the floor flies up into your face.

It is possible to make out the kid breathing heavily and Ruth sobbing quietly next to him. The gunshot has woken up Bradshaw but he's completely incoherent. You sit back down and wipe sweat from your head with your forearm.

"I've got an idea!" the kid yells in your direction and you remove your jacket. It fits over Bradshaw like a makeshift blanket.

"What?" you ask with no clue of what to expect.

"I have an idea how we can finish this this evening but I don't think you'll like it you cowardly bastard," he says attempting to antagonise you.

"I'm all ears, young man," you reply trying to sound nonchalant.

When you stand up to identify any movement you're startled by what you see. William Dudek is stood in front of the fire he no doubt built earlier and the flames light up his athletic frame. He is topless and wearing denim trousers with blood seeping from his left thigh and his gun is perched inside the front of his jeans. Ruth Coleridge is kneeling down to the left of the kid.

"Please, Bill!" she pleads with floods of tears pouring down her cheeks. Dudek ignores her protestations and focuses all his attention on the pile of coal about twenty metres away.

"Come and get me!" he screams with a maniacal grin on his face made more vivid by the raising flames behind him. You rub your face with both hands and nod your head in resignation. There is no alternative to the action you are about to take and Dudek knows it.

"We shouldn't be doing this, kid," you shout back attempting a final reconciliation.

"Stay down, he doesn't know you're alive," you whisper to Bradshaw and in acknowledgement he becomes silent. You examine your gun before taking a tight grip in your right hand. Any hesitation would be disastrous and you dart out from the coal and sprint towards the flames. The heart is once again beating rapidly and you raise your right arm and shoot towards the kid. He laughs his high-pitched squeal and you know you've missed badly.

William Dudek has removed the gun from his waist and is taking aim. Ruth Coleridge is screaming incessantly and thumping the earth with both fists. You're about five metres from the kid and decide to focus your aim on his heart. There is a loud crack followed by another but you're run is halted by what feels like a brick wall. You crash to the ground and attempt to raise your neck. Unfortunately, you feel sick and the neck thuds backwards. The only noise is crackling firewood and the inconsolable crying of Ruth Coleridge. It becomes impossible to keep your eyelids open and you drift into unconsciousness.

When your eyes open it's already getting lighter and hovering above you is the imposing figure of Colonel Poe.

"Welcome back to the land of the living Captain," he says assisting you into an upright position and taking special care of your left shoulder. It's tightly bound in bandages with a neatly circular bloodstain in the centre.

"Where's the kid?" you say to Poe failing to recognise his superior rank. The Colonel is still wearing the awful attire he had on when he abandoned you and the injured Bradshaw. He pulls you to your feet and again pays close attention to the shoulder.

"Follow me," he says softly and walks you gently past the dozen or so government workers. They are all wearing high visibility coats and there's an aftermath of smoke from the extinguished fire. Mr Bradshaw is sitting on a fold out chair receiving medical care and on another chair Ruth Coleridge has her head buried into her hands. There are no signs of Mr Deed, whilst Poe escorts you to the kid. William Dudek is lying flat on the ground with a small scorched bullet hole in his chest and has a peaceful blank expression on his scarred face.

"I shot him," you say in an attempt to make it seem real.

"He was a relic, Captain," Poe states seeing the pained anguish in your eyes.

"I shot him," you repeat with more remorse.

"The world no longer has a place for radical ideologies and romantic renegades. He will not be missed Captain," Poe states plainly and checks if you're paying attention before continuing,

"You've done an exceptional job neutralising William Dudek and all known associates. Ruth Coleridge is alive and in our custody. Well done," he concludes.

"What now, sir?" you ask politely.

"I suggest you take a well-earned rest, Major," he is beaming with pride and instead of resigning on principle you contemplate how much money a government Major can earn.

Part Two

Chapter 22

You peel your right cheek away from the leather sofa that you passed out on several hours before. The alcohol sweat has served as an adhesive between the hotel furniture and your skin. There is a large pre-poured glass of vodka next to your left arm, which dangles onto the pine flooring. There is a deep thumping in your ears synchronised with your heartbeat. You are still drunk but have no desire to complete the ritual dry retching that has accompanied most mornings of the last year. The drink takes seconds to gulp and you manage not to vomit, holding down what must be four generous measures of expensive polish vodka. You then remove all clothes and walk to the bathroom, pleased with this pre-emptive strike.

In the shower you feel the morning dosage take effect and let the content feeling wash over you with the hot water. It takes under ten minutes to tighten a burgundy tie under the collars of a pink linen shirt. You gather all the relevant documents required and put them into the right pocket of gleaming white linen trousers. When putting on a jacket the same colour and material as your trousers you see a coffee jar next to a mug. This was optimistic planning last night because you can't remember the last time you drank coffee in the morning.

It is just eight in the morning when you leave the hotel and begin making your way to His Majesty and French Republic's Migration Port. The nearby shop has been open for nearly two hours and you open the entrance door and walk in.

"Bonjour, monsieur," exclaims the proprietor of the small establishment. He knows your aren't French but insists on this repartee every morning. You wince with embarrassment when the portly white haired man reaches for a half bottle of vodka with no prompting. He lets out a small groan that most men over forty make when stretching uncomfortably and you see the tension between his fat back and faded black shirt. You grasp the bottle, hand him a twenty-Euro note expecting no change and slide the drink inside your trousers in one single transaction. A frail looking woman in her early seventies watches dispassionately at this behaviour. The settlement, you refuse to call it a town, is an amalgamation of French and British government workers sent here as punishment. The sight of someone buying vodka before nine in the morning would garner neither shock nor distain.

The largest building in the settlement is the Government Migration centre with four detention blocks built hastily around it. This is your destination and you stride along the wooden pavilion to where you've worked for nearly three months. The sea is relatively calm, which usually means a better survival rate for the migrants braving the long journey in make shift ships or inflatable supermarket boats.

Armed British and French government drones bark at these unfortunates for hours with occasional warning shots fired into the water. This pointless exercise then concludes with a minimum two-month stay in the detention blocks, sharing rooms with twelve other survivors. Your current position involves interviewing up to twelve migrants a day. These individuals are deemed potentially useful members of society. You have to decide whether they can make a positive contribution to any of the remaining cities in the United Kingdom.

There are a handful of armed government workers leaning over the promenade. Two of them are laughing manically and tapping each other on the shoulder. In the sea below is a large inflatable emergency float, perhaps stolen from a liner. Inside are four young men in their early twenties. Their clothes are filthy, torn, all appear sunburnt and exhausted.

"Turn round!" shouts one of the British workers.

"Piss off!" yells his colleague violently. They are both wearing the government issued pale blue shirts and navy trousers.

"Attention! Attention!" shouts one of the red uniformed Frenchmen. His fellow countryman hands him what looks like a half-finished bottle of red wine, which he duly drinks before wiping his sweat-ridden brow.

"Gauche! Gauche!" he continues and notices you approaching. The two British men adjust their uniforms and salute you respectfully.

"Good morning, Major," one states politely, waiting for you to respond.

"Morning, young man," you reply still unable to distinguish rank based on small details in uniform. The French are now motionless and stare at you sardonically. They are neither respectful to your rank nor intimidated by your presence. You remove a thin cigar from your jacket pocket and accept a dutiful light from one of the men. The thick smoke from your breath gathers around the eyes, whilst you observe the recent arrivals to these shores.

The migrants look like recently corned prey and their faces are gaunt. The ragged clothes hang loosely upon the emaciated bodies. One of them is gesturing for food by shovelling non-existent crumbs into his mouth. The smallest of the group is laid across the middle of their vessel groaning.

"Fermez la bouche!" shouts the Frenchmen grasping the wine before turning back to observe you cautiously.

"D'où viennent-ils?" you ask the youngest of the Gallic cousins. Unfortunately, both Frenchmen seem more fascinated by your clothing. The jaded wine connoisseur is scanning your attire from the shoulders of your jacket to the shoes and seems particularly fascinated by the shirt, pointing at it with his free hand. They are both laughing uproariously and your heavy head has had enough of this ill-advised fashion critique.

You grab the nearest French guard and remove the bottle from his hand then thump it into his stomach. He attempts to retaliate by swiping back with his gun, but you again disarm him and knock him unconscious onto the dock. His companion makes a counter attack onto your back squeezing his gun round your neck. He's extremely light but is trying to apply the maximum amount of pressure. You notice the two British guards looking on with mild amusement and you grin back sardonically. Noticing that he is till astride over your shoulders, you decide to lean backwards onto the dock and descend rapidly. There is a small cracking noise when you feel him hit the floor, using him to cushion the blow.

"Merde!" he yells in agony. After this you check yourself for any injuries, but apart from bruising on the right hand you are relatively unscathed.

You then raise yourself to your feet and observe the two Frenchmen wreathing in pain. You reach for the remnants of the bottle of wine and consume the contents with gusto. The migrants are screaming excitedly like you're here to rescue them from their insidious plight. You smile back like a triumphant gladiator. It's only when you turn round and notice the British guards are aiming guns at you that the mood sours.

"Please place both hands in the air, sir," one says calmly.

"This has to be reported, sir. It's simply too risky for the Sergeant and I to let this go. We'd be stripped of rank, perhaps worse," his fellow soldier continues.

You slowly raise both arms and attempt to muster as much dignity as possible in the process. It is another incident in a catalogue of drink-fuelled stupidity that has happened in the last year. There is no need to feel anger at these officious young men pointing firearms at an ill-disciplined, obviously drunk and overpaid Major.

"I completely understand, gentlemen," you reply allowing them to attach restraints on your wrists whilst the migrants jeer.

Chapter 23

When the now sore eyes open, you're struck by a feeling of confinement above mere incarceration. After a few moments it becomes clear that the long sheets of wood above indicate that you are slumped on the bottom of a bunk bed. It takes a few moments to adjust the body upright, carefully navigating your head under the planks. The whole of your left arm feels strained and the fingers of your left hand have already begun to tremble. The immediate solution is to take a large gulp from the vodka still in your possession. The drink itself tastes vile, but despite nearly retching, you hold down the remaining contents then return to a recovery position on the bed.

After passing in and out of sleep for about thirty minutes, blissfully letting the alcohol blot out the reality of your plight, you hear talking outside the cell door. The first voice sounds high-pitched and deferential to whomever they are talking to. The second, you instantly recognise and sigh heavily as the door opens.

"I sent you here to dry up," Colonel Poe states authoritatively.

"I'm aware of that, sir," you reply cautiously and then sit up as straight as you can manage in this delicate state. He turns back to the man keeping the door ajar, frowns and nods. The man takes the subtle signal from Poe and closes the door to leave you in private. Colonel Poe is wearing black linen trousers held up over a thin white shirt by garish deep purple braces. You follow his brown loafers as he walks across the room and slides a chair next to the bunk bed. His ample frame looks comical in the metal chair, the gargantuan thighs hanging over both sides of the seat. Once he's seated you stare hypnotically at his silk socks, which are the same colour as the braces. His eccentric clothing distracts you from your racing mind and the increasing pain in the right hand.

"What's going to happen, sir?" you ask pitifully, running the uninjured left hand over the top of your shaved head. He nods sympathetically and produces a silver hip flask from his pocket.

"First of all drink this," he states calmly and you clasp the cold silver plated flask and take a large gulp of what tastes like bourbon.

"Keep going," he says without any malice and you drink the remnants of what is a beautifully crafted flask. He stares at you like a Doctor waiting for a patient's anaesthetic to take hold.

"You've been demoted Captain," he states calmly with no hint of apology and you nod back relieved. Poe always starts conversations off with the worst news. It seems there will be no jail term.

"It could have been far worse. The Chief Guard Co-ordinator wanted you locked up as a deterrent to others. Fortunately, I explained what an important figure in His Majesty's Government you were. I pointed out how carrying out the sensitive tasks we require sometimes made you ill," he says, whilst placing the flask back in his pocket.

"Ill?" you ask sheepishly.

"Yes. You are ill Captain and I've made several arrangements for you to undergo rehabilitation," he continues, returning to his more authoritative tone.

"I'm not sure that's necessary, sir," you reply.

"You're going Captain. This is non-negotiable!" he barks back immediately before you attempt to bargain with him.

"You do understand?" he enquires in a more sympathetic way.

"I understand," you say and then sigh heavily putting your head into both hands.

"It's very fortunate that the media stationed here are usually drunker than you. The French have no desire to pursue these matters further and therefore the incident is closed. In fact Captain, it never happened," he grins ruefully.

"What about the migrants?" you ask.

"A government translator has politely explained that if they wish to seek solace in our country then their mouths will remain firmly shut," he replies then pats you on the knee and gestures for you to follow him out of the cell.

"What about assignments?" you plead, desperately trying to entangle yourself from the inevitable outcome of this discussion.

"Let me worry about your assignments. We are to leave here immediately on the transportation I arrived on. Lieutenant Wraith is waiting for us both with a government doctor," his voice is reassuring and you have no energy left to argue.

It's a relief to know Matt Wraith has joined the Colonel. You've worked with him twice on two difficult assignments and you like him. The first one was about a month after the incident with the kid. Thinking of it as an incident makes it seem less like you killed a friend. Wraith and yourself had been asked to make a routine check on some Spanish migrants who were allegedly producing illegal high volume alcohol in the basement of some capsule apartments.

It turned out that out that there was no alcohol, but in fact four heavily armed men who had kidnapped a Government Minister's ten-year-old daughter. The assailants were all killed and the girl unharmed with Wraith and yourself hailed by the media as heroes of the hour. This got Wraith promoted and you were both assigned to a straightforward surveillance operation, which lasted three months. The assignment consisted of following a high-ranking Minister's teenage son around the city's more diverse night spots and making sure he didn't, as Poe put it at the time, 'compromise His Majesty's Government'.

Wraith has a dry sense of humour and is, more importantly, excellent at what he does. You both enjoyed following the errant youngster from one bar or nightclub to another. The amount you were consuming by this point meant you could conceal it well by steadily drinking through the night, and topping yourself up back at your apartment.

The troubles really started when you returned to regular hours at work. You'd wake up with your head racing; visions of the kid, Pete Baker, or just worries and anxiety would rise up through your arms and into your chest. Then you'd grab the nearest available drink, usually next to your bed and the anxiety would dissipate in minutes. At work when your body began to anticipate the dry retching, you'd grab a leather bag from under the desk. In it, were government documents, written testimonies, witness accounts and a half bottle of vodka.

In the locked disabled toilets you'd desperately try to hold down a large enough swill without vomiting, which grew increasingly difficult. But if you managed to keep it down, you could return to the desk and complete by then the minimum amount of work possible. The vodka, allied with large doses of mouthwash or toothpaste meant you went largely unnoticed. When you fell asleep at your desk and became overly aggressive in one too many interrogations, Poe finally stepped in. He ordered you to His Majesty and French Republic's Migration Port for a 'rest'.

Colonel Poe helps you step onto the ship like you're a frail elderly man and there to greet you are, a miniscule man, who you assume is the Doctor and Matt Wraith. Matt is tanned and muscular wearing a red polo shirt, khaki trousers and sockless loafers. He holds out his hand with no prejudice or judgement and you shake it.

"Hello Major, or is it Captain now?" he asks sarcastically.

"I still out rank you," you reply and smile back. He pats you on the back and introduces you to the Medic.

"Look after him Doctor, he's getting old," says Wraith.

Chapter 24

The first night was the worst, and you barely slept two hours. When the effects of the vodka wore off you could feel the terror cloak your body. The anxiety flooded down along your arms, leaving you fearful of a heart attack. The constant worry about your breathing and belief was there that if you close your eyes you wouldn't wake. The Doctor refused to prescribe anything to wean your body off the alcohol, instead favouring isolation in a hospital room, sweating out the poison.

The next day you vaguely remember trying to escape the hospital, sprinting down the ward corridor only to be met by a prototype security guard made from concrete. Having pinned you to the floor the young man then escorted you back to your room. At night the overwhelming sense of futility drained you to the point of exhaustion, but every thought you had would be tinged with negativity, which lead to panic.

On the second day you remember waking, disappointed that the dark thoughts were still dominating your jaded mind. You tried to distract yourself with books, turning pages without reading or listening to music. Finally after days you managed to hold down food without vomiting it back up. The constant knowledge that one large glass of vodka would quell your mind and bodies' unrest left you feeling helpless.

The third day you woke after another night's broken sleep feeling slightly less pitiful, but still drenched in sweat. You have never felt so ashamed, destitute and negative in your life, weeping tears sporadically all day. After another night of sleep deprivation you plead with the doctor that he gives you something to help sleep. He obliges and nods at the nurse, who brings two-minute white pills that you swallow down rapidly with no water.

In no more than ten minutes you begin to feel the anxiety lift and the minds decreasing it's whirlwind like pace. You giggle with relief out loud before turning on your side and fall into a blissful sleep. When you wake the feeling of sickness has dissipated and you feel numb. The doctor encourages you to walk about, convincing you that the worst is over.

Even in the midst of an acute drinking session you weighed yourself daily, a strangely vain routine in the circumstances. When you step on the hospital scales in the room you notice you've lost 3kg in five days and look at the shadowy presence in the mirror.

It was on the sixth day during the afternoon that Matt Wraith insisted on taking you to the hospital gym. You felt pitifully weak when attempting to lift weights that previously presented no problems. Matt patiently urged you on with each passing visit, slowly increasing the amount of weights you lifted.

After two weeks you caught yourself smiling ruefully, not at any huge sense of achievement. It was just the recognition that you'd had a positive thought, which seemed an impossibility days before. The mind still raced with self-doubt and guilt and occasionally you'd wake up early drenched in sweat. There was still the sick anxiety in the pit of your stomach but it had become manageable. After twenty-one days the hospital released you back into society looking physically, if not mentally healthy.

The apartment is immaculate today, which it remained even in your heaviest drinking bouts. You remember waking after a serious drinking bout surrounded by freshly washed and ironed clothes that you'd no recollection of preparing. The large mirror above your bookcase still looms over the oak bookcase and you observe the reflection critically.

You slide the palm of the right hand across three days of stubble and stare intently at yourself. When you left the hospital yesterday you were measured at 183cm and weighed just less than 82 kilograms. You are still tanned from your brief tenure at the migration port and the weights sessions have left you looking refreshed. The slim lined navy polo shirt hangs over your lean muscular physique. In the pocket of your khaki trousers you unfold the letter that arrived from Poe on the evening of your last day in the hospital. The letter is concise but heartfelt and states,

'Glad you're feeling better. Please come to my office on Thursday after 10am. I have an assignment that may interest you. Poe'

His handwriting is amusingly infantile but you feel a wave of gratitude to the Colonel. It's five past nine in the morning when you step onto the streets below your apartment and the trams still looked crushed with commuters. Poe's office is based in 'The Department for Immigration and Environment' on the fifth floor. It's only about three miles away and you opt to walk there.

The sky is a cloudless aqua blue and the temperature is souring. This would normally lead to incessant alcohol sweats from every pore of your body; instead you enjoy the pleasant sea breeze that sweeps over your shaved palate. You pull the collar of your red polo shirt and fan your chest. A tall ginger haired man, complete with matching beard is stood on the pavement covered in sweat. He's wearing an ill fitted white shirt over his obese frame and his linen blue jacket is two sizes larger than necessary. There is a media indistinguishable media logo on the lapel and he is holding a large mass of newspapers, which you duly take.

The main headline is a stereotypical moral panic about the decline of national identity. The sport pages are dominated by a nostalgic piece on the pleasures of watching cricket, a sport no longer played during the day because of the intense heat. On the inside you see an athletics star grasping a large bottle of champagne, which sets the mind racing and you throw the paper in the nearest bin.

Its fifteen minutes past ten when you arrive at 'The Department for Immigration and Environment' and after handing your identification to a barrel-chested security guard the main door is opened. The corridor floors are immaculately clean and you feel self-conscious at the noise your shoes make when they make contact. The fifth floor has only three occupied offices, all situated on the right hand side of the corridor. Poe's is the closest to the stairwell and has a large oak door, with the Colonel's name printed in a clear font in capitals. You knock twice on the freshly polished door.

"Enter!" Poe yells rather regally and you walk in. He is sitting behind a transparent glass table propped up by silver plated legs. The Colonel is dressed in a pale blue cotton suit with a bright red tie, which is reflecting the sun from the nearest window. He seems startled by your presence, and gets up from his chair to greet you.

"Do you have another appointment, sir?" You politely enquire. There is a genuine grin on the face of your superior officer.

"Nothing of any consequence, Captain," he states reassuringly before squeezing the biceps on your right arm.

"Lieutenant Wraith promised to begin putting you through a regime. They say that there are places for you to visit too. Meeting places." The tone is awkward and you attempt to reassure him.

"There are meetings, sir. I've been to a few already and they've given me a greater sense of clarity," you state calmly. You don't mention the constant dreams of drinking you've had repeatedly at night.

"Well quite," he replies, still somewhat reticently before offering you a seat on the other side of his desk.

"Are you ready to work, Captain?" he asks generously.

"Yes, sir," you respond emphatically.

"I think this assignment will appeal to the more inquisitive aspects of your character," he says mischievously and slides a folder marked confidential along the desk.

"Thank you, Colonel."

Chapter 25

The photo is approximately a decade old, but the face hasn't changed and the only difference is the hairstyle. The iconic shaved head is years away, replaced here by expensively treated strands of black hair greased back over a tanned forehead. The file has his height at 188cm but he appears taller in the picture. He's stood next to a small boy who is beaming with pride and holding a tenant aloft. The man is aged thirty-four at this time and dressed superbly in slim fit beige trousers, sky blue shirt and a hand-made navy waistcoat. He has no tie with the top two buttons of his shirt undone revealing a waxed chest.

"According to his birth certificate Sir Terence Armstrong is forty-five years of age. It's never been confirmed where he was born," Poe states.

"His mystery has always been part of his appeal, sir," you reply.

"Yes Captain, he's quite the media darling," the Colonel retorts.

"Apparently, the business he brings to the islands is keeping the country economically afloat. He's done a great deal for the city too, with migration. With his beautiful wife, three children and personal relationship with the King, he's untouchable. They went to the same school apparently."

"That is why you will be conducting this assignment in the full knowledge of Sir Terence. His organisation contacted us through a third party confirming this two days ago."

"What is the assignment? There are no instructions in the file Colonel," you plead with him.

"From a government perspective Sir Terence Armstrong is a bastion of the city community, however if you wouldn't mind looking at the final photo in the file. It's black and white I'm afraid, but quite clear," he says, gazing down on the opened folder.

The photo you remove is about the size of an old postcard. Sir Terence Armstrong is sitting at a beachside café sipping an espresso. Sitting opposite him, with a tall thin glass of beer is William Dudek. You can feel the same dry sickening feeling in your stomach that you've felt frequently over the past year. The Doctors in the hospital informed you that this was alcoholic gastritis and after the detoxification such feelings would dissipate.

"What do you make of that?" Poe enquires coldly. You stare at the photo but remain silent.

"It is important that we find out why these two gentlemen were acquaintances. Armstrong has no idea that this identification exists and we would prefer he remains unaware. This matter has to be dealt with finesse and guile. As you rightly asserted, Sir Terence is a respected and powerful man," he informs you tactfully.

"How old is the photograph?" you ask abruptly.

"It was taken a month before Dudek's death by Lieutenant Wraith. I would like you to speak with him tomorrow morning before your meeting with Sir Terence," his voice is calm and measured.

"Yes, sir," you mutter incoherently with your eyes still fixed on the photo.

"Wraith will be assisting you in the early stages of this investigation. He's made contact with Armstrong's personal assistant and will brief you on the relevant details in the morning. His office is situated on the third floor of this building."

"Do I still report to you, Colonel?" you ask, still bewildered and feeling nauseous.

"Yes. This is your new firearm and I need you to sign this paper," he points his right index to an administrative document and you sign it dutifully.

"I wouldn't have selected you for this case Captain, unless I had confidence in your ability and tenacity to discover the true nature of this unlikely friendship between Dudek and Armstrong," he states before holding out his hand, which you grasp firmly.

"Good luck, Captain," the Colonel says.

"Thank you, sir," you reply despondently and then leave the room swiftly.

In the elevator, your mind is racing and the legs feel weakened and fragile. The image of the kid sat opposite Armstrong continues to resurface into your thoughts and the eardrums beat to the rhythm of your relentlessly thumping heart. The fingertips are numb like they were during an epic-drinking bout. On the street outside the government buildings you feel disassociated and distant. The only way you've ever dealt with this horrendous feeling in the past is to drink but you try the mental techniques you've been told.

You remember the tortuous emotions and negative thoughts as your body sweated the alcohol out over the course of five days. You recall the uncontrollable shakes and the ineffectiveness drink had now on altering the way you felt. The anxiety swept over your nerves sporadically in waves and all because you are an alcoholic. This acceptance is calming and you begin walking back towards your apartment. It is difficult to walk past the hordes of workers enjoying a dinnertime beer with their food but you know the eventual results.

There is a small café about ten minutes from your apartment where you order a hot chocolate and take a seat at a single table. You open the file Poe gave you and light a cigar with a wafer fin lighter. The photo of the kid and Armstrong is firmly at the bottom of the files and documents. The one thousand-word dossier on Sir Terence is concise and informative.

The first paragraph speculates on his potential birthplace, whether it was Scotland or as most sources suggest the northern islands of England. He is the only child of Christina and Paul Armstrong, a successful government official who was elevated to the role of Private Secretary of the late former King. This is where the young Terence became friends with the current monarch at several elite public schools.

For the first three decades of his life Terence Armstrong travelled the world working on several charity projects in the countries, most severely affected by the climate changes. He was working on reconstruction work in Iceland when he inherited his father's fortune, with Paul dying of a heart condition when Terence was a month from his thirtieth birthday.

It was then that he moulded his image in the media as the successful businessman, making billions of Euro dollars on new housing for the increasingly cramped city migrants. He managed to combine this lucrative scheme with high profile charity work and even helped the government backed 'frugality' campaign. Armstrong championed a society where its members would save at least a fifth of their monthly income, recycle everything possible and cut back on needless spending. For example shaving his hair as a symbol of this 'frugal metropolis'.

His private life has been impeccable and he married his childhood sweetheart Marie at the age of thirty-three in a low profile wedding in France. A close friend of the King, he became Sir Terence Armstrong before turning forty. The dossier concludes by explaining how his reputation is entirely untarnished and his company continues to thrive despite the uncertain economic climate.

You pour a small amount of pouring cream into the piping hot chocolate and place the photo of Dudek and Sir Terence on top of the other documents. It makes no sense why the privileged billionaire and a knight of his majesty's realm are sat opposite a renowned counter government agent and member of the dwindling cause. However there he is, contently sipping a coffee in the midday sun with the late William Dudek.

"Can I get a bill for this please? I'll need the receipt too," you politely ask the young waiter.

Chapter 26

It's a beautiful morning when you wake up with the sunlight illuminating the apartment. It's just past six and you swallow the medication that the hospital advised you to consume daily. One of the pills flushes your body leaving you with a temporary bright red face. After about ten minutes you stop looking like a pensioner who's fallen asleep in the sun and feel invigorated. You have noticed how calm you feel when you've attended a meeting the previous evening. Every meeting is reassuringly similar in format and you experience the same mild euphoria akin to a gym training session.

The appointment at the Armstrong Head Office in the city centre is at midday, so decide on a fresh shave. You stare back at the tanned complexion in the mirror and notice the white hair flecks near your temples. They are barely noticeable when your head is freshly shaved but you've deliberately let it grow out. After a rapid shower you are dressed within ten minutes. You're wearing slim fit khaki trousers, white cotton shirt with a plain yellow tie and pale blue linen waistcoat. The heat seems intense outside and you slip into sockless black tassel loafers, which you polished therapeutically last night.

Matt is waiting for you at 'Café Lorient' a new continental style breakfast bar. It's only seven o'clock in the morning but it is already vibrant. A young man in his early twenties is sitting in salmon shorts and a Breton top smoking seriously at a single table. Two women in their thirties are occupying the table next to this youngster, sipping hot chocolate. The first woman has her hair tied up with a chopstick through the middle and is listening intently. Her companion, a petite attractive woman with red lipstick on, is gesticulating wildly with her hands. Behind both of these tables is Matt Wraith stirring a large black coffee.

"How are mate?" he stands aloft and holds out his hand.

"I'm good, Matt," you reply and give his hand a firm shake.

Matt gestures to the waiter, who quickly returns with your order of a hot chocolate. You place the foreign cigars that Matt Wraith brought back from an assignment in what is left of Kyoto.

"I've not had one of these yet. Will you join me?" you enquire.

"It's seven in the morning," he laughs but accepts one from the brown and cream cigar box.

"I'll have this later," Matt says sliding it in the inside pocket of his navy jacket.

You light the cigar and blow the sweet tasting tobacco from your lips.

"I find I'm smoking more of these at the moment," you stare at the cigar like an exhibit.

"It could be worse I suppose. You saw the photo then?" he asks.

"Yes. Poe showed it to me," your tone is cold.

"It was a separate operation to your assignment. We knew about your investigation, but we were to follow a small group of them; Pete Baker, Dudek and even that lunatic Makowski."

"I understand, Matt," you reply with genuine warmth.

"You wouldn't believe the things that Mak would get up to in the evening. Well, maybe you would," he laughs nervously but any air of tension has gone.

"We had explicit instructions not to get involved, no matter how horrific the incidents we witnessed. The Colonel made it clear there would be no interference," Matt continues becoming more animated.

"Where was that photo taken," you enquire.

"Near the coast, with those rejuvenated beaches. It's where the students have barbeques and play beach football. They leave bottles of beer everywhere, like a dumping ground. We'd followed the kid here from some strange new age lodge about an hour from the city. The kid and some bloke with white hair sat on the beach naked for hours. They'd occasionally run into the sea for a swim but most of the time sat upright, with their legs crossed. We'd be hid away taking pictures. Very strange," you smile at this information and gesture for Matt to continue.

"Eventually the kid made his farewells to this older man and ended up on these city beaches. He spent the next week staying at small hotel on the coast. During the day the kid would sit meditating, before drinking in the evening," Wraith explains with care.

"What about Terence Armstrong?" you ask intrigued by this narrative.

"That was an interesting day. The kid had been drinking since nine in the morning slowly, sipping a thin glass of beer. After he ordered the fourth or fifth, two men sat at the table where Dudek was cradling his drink. The first man was a colossus of just under two metres in height. The other man was an immaculately dressed tall man, brandishing sunglasses. Only this man and the kid spoke, the other stepping away from the table after a few minutes," he continues.

"Did the conversation seem genial?" you interrupt.

"They obviously knew each other. There wasn't any knee slapping or uncontrollable laughter but they'd met before. It was my assistant on the assignment that recognised Armstrong; Alan Miles, from the deportation department. A real pain in the arse but recognised him instantly. Once Poe received my report, I was called into his office. After what happened to the kid," he pauses solemnly and you urge him to continue.

"After the kid died we were sworn to secrecy by Poe. He threatened to send me where you ended up herding migrants off inflatable boats," Matt begins laughing uncontrollably smacking his hand onto the table.

"What does the company know?" you ask conspiratorially

"Nothing. They're expecting a government official to turn up and compile a report on the smooth running of the Armstrong brand. Anyone who works so closely with the government on social policy expects some scrutiny. It's standard procedure," he assures you.

"Thanks, Matt," you say sensing his desire to get to work on time.

"Not a problem, sir," he replies sarcastically giving you a salute.

"I won't keep you any longer Sergeant. I know Colonel Poe likes his morning coffee served piping hot," you respond.

"You look after yourself, mate," he pats you on the back and walks away to the nearest tram stop.

The Armstrong Head Office is only about a ten-minute walk from 'Café Lorient', which means there is time to order breakfast. You ask for some well-done bacon on toast, a large glass of squeezed orange juice and a black coffee.

The toasted bread has been sliced thickly from an oven-baked loaf and you spread on generous portions of butter between the crisp bacon slices. You have to ask for the bacon to be well done or it is barely cooked at all. After paying the bill you decide to walk through the city shopping districts.

The shops have been open for well over an hour and most have several customers inside trying on clothes. You browse round new Japanese tailors on the main high street. There is a beautifully designed folder with the fabrics inside and you decide to order a pale blue linen suit after being measured by an assistant. You pay in the store and make you way back into the street. A bearded man bumps into you swigging from a small bottle of gin.

"Do you want some, mate?" he slurs offering you the bottle.

"No thanks," you reply.

Your mind begins to race obsessively about alcohol and the anxiety levels rise. You remember someone at a meeting mentioned playing out where this narrative leads. The last ended with you wrestling drunken French soldiers, dry retching in a cell. This thought calms you and you sit back down in 'Café Lorient' and order a hot chocolate.

Chapter 27

The Armstrong Head Office is an imposing building situated in the business quarter of the city. Hordes of slickly suited males storm past you, all with an air of urgency. On the front of the ten storey's building is the five-metre high symbol of Armstrong's corporation. A gigantic mint green letter 'A' encased in a circular amalgamation of the European countries flags. It's a simple but striking image, apparently designed by Sir Terence himself; the intentional colour of the letter and the harmony between the European states encompassing the Armstrong vision.

The tiles and pillars of the ground floor entrance are polished and immaculate. You listen to the noise the shoes make on the surface as you step towards the reception desk. There is an extremely attractive women in her late twenties sat in a leather chair, behind a transparent desk. On the wall behind her is one of the new holographic fish tanks that you read about in the hospital. The fish and the texture of the water change every thirty seconds.

"I don't suppose you have to feed them do you?" you say to the woman.

"That's certainly not an issue, sir," she replies looking you up and down before smiling back generously.

"I have an appointment at midday with Mr Armstrong," you tell the young lady handing her your appointment and identification cards. She has her peroxide hair tied back and is wearing a slim line black dress. The face is tanned and freckled on her forehead above the brown eyes. There are wrinkles around her eyes, which only increase her appeal.

"Yes. I'll let Mr Boland know you've arrived," she replies salaciously.

"Mr Boland?" you enquire politely

"Mr Boland is in charge of Marketing Strategies and assists any individuals conducting external investigations. He's our resident public relations man too," she responds rapidly. You watch her type something into a pale green laptop and she gestures for you to sit on a sofa opposite the desk.

"Is everything here pale green?" you comment on the colour of the seating.

"He'll be with you in five minutes, sir," she states with finality and then continues typing into her laptop. You lean back into the sofa and cross your leg over the opposing knee examining the leather soles of your loafers. There are still marks scattered over the soles, which you achieved with a small nail. In retrospect a good idea or the faultless flooring would have felt like an ice rink. The doors behind the secretary slide open and a man of just less than six foot walks through confidently. He is wearing a light grey suit, white shirt, red tie and black brogue shoes. The man seems to be in his late thirties, has shortly cropped jet-black hair, and ill-advised shaped eyebrows. The hand is held out and you rise from your seat squeezing it firmly.

"I do hope you haven't been waiting long Captain. If you'll follow me this way, we can begin a brief tour of our offices. Would you care for a drink?" his voice is insincere and he adopts a ghastly grin, whilst leading you back through the sliding doors.

"I'm fine thank you. I had some coffee before arriving," you reply dutifully.

"She's quite something isn't she?" he winks at you and looks back towards the secretary. The grin is now replaced with an equally disturbing lecherous stare.

"She seems lovely," you reply diplomatically.

"My name is Damian Boland and I'm here to assist you with any enquiries that you may have during this investigation. The last gentlemen who visited us from the government was a wonderful chap called Wright, do you know him?" he asks enthusiastically.

"It's a very large department and our remits constantly change. I've been abroad for a number of months," you reply watching him type in a security code to another locked door.

"Anywhere pleasant?" he asks with feigned interest.

"France," you reply dryly. Mr Boland ignores this reply and continues his tour.

"I thought I'd show you how our operation here is run and then we've scheduled an appointment with Mr Armstrong for ten past one," he continues as you follow him into an elevator. All the numbered buttons in the lift are pale green with the company logo on the wall adjacent. Boland presses the number three and waits. The doors open to reveal an open plan area dominated by large comfortable chairs and laptops.

"This is our advertising department," he holds out his arm dramatically.

There are about twenty people stood up wandering around holding various documents or pieces of paper. About a dozen are huddled together over laminated green tables debating in small groups. One individual is making wild gestures with his hands. Only a handful of people are sat behind laptops typing furiously. Everyone appears to be under the age of thirty and is dressed casually. Most of the men are wearing denim and highly coloured t-shirts, whereas the young women are dressed in either the French or Japanese fashion. All the ladies hair is either cropped short and dyed or tied up held together with chopsticks.

"They might look very young Captain, but these are the most talented copyrighters in the city. Sir Armstrong believes its essential our message is presented in an attractive but assessable way," says Boland.

"Message?" you ask quixotically.

"The Armstrong foundation prides itself on helping to create an environmentally friendly city, which can incorporate all elements into our diverse community," he informs you, sounding like a politician giving a campaign promise.

He stands with his arms folded beaming with pride at the activity we're witnessing. He walks you over to a scale model of a proposed block of capsule apartments.

"This is their brief at the moment. Not the cramped spaces and rabid violence associated with capsule apartments. These will be more like luxurious families' homes for migrants who want to contribute to our growing city," he is still grinning inanely as he hovers over two youngsters scribbling on notepaper.

"I'll take you to the fifth floor. You won't believe what the set-up is like there," he says proudly.

"Is it green?" you ask sarcastically.

"Please follow me, Captain," he replies deadpan. You follow him back into the lift and you stand together silently as the lift moves up two floors.

The fifth floor is incredibly noisy with hundreds of desks neatly placed side by side, resembling a school exam hall. It's mostly women sat behind green painted pine desks. The employees all have earphones in and appear to be talking to people on the laptop screens. Boland stares at you intently and you nod mischievously at the green desks. He feigns amusement and continues the tour.

"This is where we deal with the numerous charities that Sir Terence has founded. The ladies could be talking to a new migrant seeking refuge, students making enquiries about funding and sometimes generous individuals wishing to contribute financially," he smiles at a middle-aged woman speaking in a soft tone into her laptop.

"It really is a wonderful thing we do here," Boland gushes unapologetically walking you onwards.

"I'll take you to the staff rooms now. This will give you a chance to interact with our employees before meeting Sir Terence," he says.

"I'd like to have a look at the other floors too," you state clearly. He stops and pauses to reflect, looking anxious.

"Come along, Captain. I have staff waiting for us."

Chapter 28

The pre-arranged meeting with staff is excruciating and the ingratiating Boland hovering over proceedings. You are seated on a staff dinner table with four employees. There are two startled looking youngsters in their early twenties and two middle aged men. One of these men expounds the joys of the company pension he's accrued over twenty years. The other sits staring into the distance with deep apathy for the whole laborious process. Finally after fifteen minutes, Damian Boland makes sure the meeting finishes punctually. He then walks you purposively to Sir Terence Armstrong's main office. There is a waiting room outside with a large chesterfield sofa, which you sit on.

"I'll just see if Sir Terence is available," says Boland and opens the main door.

"The gentleman from the government has arrived Sir Armstrong," you hear the subservient tones through the thin wooden door. Damian Boland pokes his head out of the door and smiles.

"He's ready for you, Captain," he says ushering you inside with extravagant hand movements.

The room is spacious but devoid of much interior design and there are only three pictures on the walls. The largest is an immaculately framed photo of Armstrong, his glamorous wife and three children. Sir Armstrong is stood over his traditional oak desk, leaning over it with his left hand. In the right hand is a recently lit seven-inch cigar omitting thick white smoke. He begins walking towards you with his hand held out, which you shake firmly.

"Thank you for agreeing to speak with me Sir Armstrong," you state courteously.

"It's a pleasure, Captain," he smiles broadly, which causes his eyes to squint. He is dressed in tailored black trousers, a pale green shirt with button down collars and beautifully polished black shoes. He is well over six foot, with a slim but athletic frame and the hair is freshly shaved.

"I'm not sure I believe that, Sir Armstrong," you respond ruefully.

"Please take a seat," he offers you a seat near his desk. After sitting down you observe his actions and notice a two-inch scar under his chin, which stands out more on his sun-tanned skin. He clenches the cigar between his teeth; inhaling and exhaling smoke rapidly like the chimneys you remember from your youth. Boland hands a small file over to Armstrong.

"That will be all, Damian. Thank you," Sir Terence says warmly to his subordinate, who quietly leaves the room. You take your seat and notice faint meditation music in the background.

"Do you like the music?" he asks, noticing your interest.

"Yes. I'm trying to meditate every morning," you reply truthfully.

"It's an essential part of my day. I've been doing meditation and breathing practice for the last ten years. It unclutters my mind and helps me focus on my goals for day," he outlines.

"It's obviously working, Sir Terence. This is quite an operation you have here," you say politely, mindful of how much you dislike it when individuals refer to their 'goals'

"Do you practice breathing?" he enquires.

"No. I've been okay with my breathing for nearly four decades now," you respond sarcastically. He laughs uproariously and hits the expensive oak table he's sitting behind.

"I'd give it a try Captain. These things don't help!" he looks up at his cigar and laughs again.

"I'm an amalgamation of contradictions you see," he continues, staring at you intensely through the smoke. Sir Terence's attire is exquisitely simple; the high-heeled boot adds an inch to his already considerable frame. The wafer thin gold watch on his left wrist looks beautifully constructed.

"What do you mean?" you ask.

"I've actively funded and took part in government campaigns set up to improve health. Running in the cooler morning air, cleaning out the waste in the sea for swimmers and building all those air-conditioned football courts I built in deprived areas. And yet here I am surrounding myself in cigar smoke." He informs you and then laughs out loud again. It's an ingratiating shrill noise and you understand why he rarely laughs in public. His public relations and marketing teams have probably advised him to keep his mouth closed. Sir Terence opens the file that Boland handed him and begins reading it.

"It says in the file that you're here for a routine surveillance of our company. How long do you expect this to take?" he lifts his eyes up from the report.

"A maximum of three days," you reply.

"That seems reasonable Captain. We completely understand how important it is for the Government to monitor such a high profile organisation. Especially considering the criticisms heaped on the various departments recently," his eyes narrow and he waits for your response expectantly.

"Criticisms?" you ask earnestly.

"The appalling way migrants are dealt with, millions of Euros wasted, criminal subcultures and an inactive government cabinet. You and I are old enough to remember when we had leaders. Presidents and Prime Ministers with real substance behind their words," he argues passionately.

"I think they're doing an extremely difficult job rather well Sir Terence. I'm quite surprised such a high profile supporter of government schemes feels so vociferously," you reply diplomatically.

"The country requires active role models. I didn't shave my hair off as a publicity stunt or for vanity. I'm trying to highlight areas where we could all be more frugal," he continues as you notice a beam of light reflect from his gold timepiece.

"It's possible to have leaders who aren't tyrants or dictators," he points out.

"A charismatic businessman perhaps?" you reply wistfully. He grins broadly and stubs out his cigar into a metal ashtray on the table.

"You are quite right Captain. The vast majority of problems in our city are dealt with effectively. I simply feel that there are better ways of approaching things like migration. For example, look at the dreadful way border control is managed. Don't you have personal experience of this Captain?" his tone is aggressive and the eyes stare at you with menace. You feel the anxiety rise up from your stomach and along the arms. The heart is pumping dramatically through your ribcage. The mind begins to race and you speculate how he could possibly know about the incident in France.

"Yes. I've worked on the borders," you reply cordially.

"I had heard something about your work there," Terence Armstrong's tone is more relaxed.

"There is one question I have for you Sir Terence," you state humbly.

"What is it, Captain?" he asks, smiling generously again.

"Have you ever met a man called William Dudek?" you say coldly. His tanned face turns ashen and he rubs his shaved head softly.

"I read about him," he replies, trying to gain his composure.

"Did you meet him?" you enquire.

"No. Never. I wish you good luck with your investigation Captain. Please don't hesitate to ask for any assistance. Could you ask Mr Boland to come back in on your way out?" The colour has returned to his face but he still seems perturbed.

"Yes. It's been a pleasure meeting you Sir Terence," you tell him and leave the room feeling the anxiety dissipating.

Chapter 29

The anxiety soon returns when you leave the building, it rises up through both arms and the head goes cold. You are consumed by fear and the mind begins to race thunderously. Your heart is beating quickly against the chest and unwanted thoughts enter the mind rapaciously; the kid, Sir Terence, the meaningless of everything, passing out, Boland's sycophancy, having a heart attack and intense fear of death. Previously a drink would alleviate this acute sense dread, but that's no longer an option.

You breathe slowly and try to acclimatise to where you're stood. A meeting is what's required, they always neutralise these awkward sensations. There are hundreds all over the city for nurses, doctors, and office workers, migrants, for anyone. It's one in the afternoon and a meeting in a nearby community centre has just started. You direct your body there slowly trying to block out the racing mind. It's started and you sit, you listen and you share.

The meeting lasts an hour and you leave feeling placid and serene. You light a cigar and smile knowingly at a middle-aged man in a black linen suit leaving the same gathering. It's only now that you ponder how Sir Terence responded to your question. There was immense satisfaction in denting his self-confidence, that self-effacing façade, even if it only lasted seconds. The question was reckless but it's important to see how he'll respond with this knowledge. The assignment would have been a wasted opportunity if you'd just nodded politely at your host. In emasculating Armstrong, however briefly, you now expect a reaction.

This evening you're staying at one of the city's five purpose built by Sir Terence. A needless and unwanted gesture that Colonel Poe felt had to be accepted. The Armstrong Urban Village Hotel is the closest to the main building you've just left.

It takes less than five minutes to check in at light green desk and a young man in his early twenties escorts you to the second floor room. The décor inside is sparse, in the Japanese style. There's a low-level double bed, no head post and a pine desk with a synthetic bonsai tree perched next to an information pack.

"Thank you young man," you say handing him ten-Euro dollars. He accepts the money and tries, vainly, to hide his disappointment at the meagre amount.

"Thank you, sir," he replies dryly.

"What time is the pool open?" you enquire.

"It's never closed sir. We can provide you with the necessary clothing," he responds dutifully before leaving you to prepare a small pot of tea.

There's a stunning painting of the Japanese countryside hanging on the wall. Its style is more reminiscent of artists from centuries past, rather than abstract pieces that have been in vogue for well over a hundred years. The tea is piping hot, with no milk necessary. You sit at the desk and lean back into the luxuriant burgundy armchair and sip from the china mug. On the desk you've placed the various documents and photos neatly next to each other. You grasp the photo of Armstrong and Dudek staring at the image intensely hoping to form some clarity regarding their relationship.

After playing out various scenarios on how they met, you decide to go for a swim. This has always been meditative, but became increasingly rare as your drinking escalated. It's situated underneath the ground floor and clearly sign-posted throughout the hotel. You produce guest identification for an overweight man in his early thirties. His long hair is thinning, which has produced an unfortunate island in the middle of his palate.

"Do you suffer from any heart conditions, sir?" he asks in a high-pitched tone. He's wearing an ill fitted red polo shirt and swimming shorts the same colour.

"No," you reply and grasp the swimming shorts, towel and locker key he offers.

The swimming pool is expansive and surprisingly warm. You swim for about half an hour, before pulling yourself from the water using your arms. The woman who was sitting reading, when you arrived has left and there is only yourself and a thickset man sat in the steam room. The obese lifeguard administrator has left his post at the desk and you make your way into the showers. The shower blasts on to your shaved head. It's refreshingly hot and you close your eyes peacefully and enjoy the water cascading over your body. You feel a powerful grip formed round your neck and open your eyes. There are two hirsute muscle bound arms tightly locked around your neck.

"How was your swim, dickhead?" a menacing voice whispers into your ear. The grip gets tighter and you can barely breathe but attempt to wriggle free, which is nearly impossible in bare feet on a slippery surface.

"You're not going anywhere pal. You shouldn't have tried to be a clever bastard," says the voice.

You try to get a good grasp of one of his arms but he merely tightens his grip. The wall of the showers is in front and you propel your legs and push yourself back off the wall, falling on top of the stranger. There is a sharp cracking noise and you quickly rise to your feet. He's stood up too but is holding the left side of his ribcage. You don't hesitate in seizing an advantage and punch him squarely in the right jaw, hearing a second cracking noise. He stumbles to the floor and you slowly kick him in the stomach, watching him wince in pain.

"You should have stayed in the steam room, mate," you say, hovering over his drenched and battered body. It would be a colossal waste of time interrogating him and his motives are obvious. You dab down your body with a towel, which you then throw onto his face. He coughs loudly clutching his ribcage as you calmly stroll to the changing room.

This assault was undoubtedly a personal test, after the fractious meeting with Sir Terence. They'll now know that you're not a desk bound administrator, who has become too inquisitive. The trim brute heaped on the shower tiles would only ever be used to startle civilians. Once you responded to the attack, he was too easy to neutralise as a threat. The overweight attendant is back at his post, no doubt told to make himself scarce. He face is sweat ridden and he seems anxious.

"How was the swim, sir?" he asks nervously.

"It was lovely, the temperature is just about right," you reply cheerfully.

"Were there any problems, sir?" he asks in an apprehensive tone.

"No, the facilities here are exceptional. There is something though."

"What, sir?" he says, his gaze transfixed on you.

"A rather large gentleman has slipped in the shower. He seems rather accident-prone. In fact, it looks like he's slipped more than once and is quite seriously injured," you state dryly.

"I'll deal with this immediately sir. Thank you for letting me know," he responds running his hand through his thinning hair.

When returning to the privacy of your room, you inspect the body for injuries in the bathroom mirror. There is some minor bruising around you right shoulder but nothing else. You prepare some clothes for tomorrow's meeting at The Armstrong Head Office. The small suitcase of clothes was dispatched this morning at your request and you remove some items. A lightweight slim fit grey suit, plain white shirt, burgundy braces and a knitted tie the same colour. You are scheduled to visit the construction of some luxury capsule apartments, so you leave out some freshly polished black lace-less boots. You then boil some more water for tea and sit by the desk re-examining the assignment notes.

Chapter 30

It's six o'clock when you wake up, and you step out of bed feeling refreshed. You're grateful for the seven hours sleep, because it was genuine rest. Most nights over the last year have been more tortuous, passing out on your sofa or upright in a chair, with a glass of vodka or whiskey nearby. You'd open your eyes and slip a large enough dosage down the throat before staggering to a bed. When you eventually got out of bed, you'd gulp more alcohol medicinally before showering.

No breakfast, which you couldn't hold down without a drink by that point. The dry retching would dominate the morning, until you'd held down enough vodka without vomiting. This thought makes you shudder as you tighten the burgundy tie around your neck. Then it would have been a simple process of topping yourself up throughout the day, never completely drunk but certainly not sober, before allowing yourself to unwind fully after work.

You sit calmly on the comfortable chair with both palms grasping the knees. The headphones you've put into your ears have a soft chiming music playing and you begin meditating. This would have been impossible only months ago, with a mind incapable of floating peacefully from one thought to another. It still feels faintly ridiculous, sat with your eyes closed and slowly breathing through your nose. But after just five minutes you do feel more serene and make your way downstairs for breakfast.

Having accepted a newspaper and taken a seat you wait to be served by the any of the young staff. A slim man in his early twenties marches quickly in your direction.

"What can I get you, sir?" he asks politely, with a slight eastern European accent.

"A decaf coffee with some pouring cream please, young man," you reply.

"And for breakfast, sir?" he asks, smiling pleasantly.

"I'd like some well-done bacon on brown toast and lots of butter please," you reply.

"Well done," he mumbles, whilst scribbling down the order. The coffee is brought to your table with the cream on the side in a small white cup. You pour the contents into the coffee and then take a small sip.

The front page of the newspaper is a horrific account of the beating of a nineteen-year-old student. He'd been coming back from a nightclub the previous night after escorting his girlfriend home. Four men seized him upon, only fifty yards from a tram stop. The men punched the boy to the floor and kicked him repeatedly in the head. His skull was cracked; a rib shattered and is only alive because of miraculous medical treatment. The most striking part in the article is the headline 'Sir Terence appalled by new migrant attackers' There is a five inch picture of Armstrong with his arms folded and frowning earnestly into the camera.

The story of violent migrants isn't particularly unusual, but Sir Terence commenting on the incident is. He apparently abhors violence and believes that someone needs to take a lead on migration issues. In his final statement to the paper he pleads for leadership. This seems a bizarre public statement to make, when one considers the amount of public work Armstrong does for the migrant communities.

When the food arrives you fold the newspaper and place it to one side. The toast is crisp and the bacon drenched in butter, giving it more taste. Someone is scheduled to meet you outside the hotel at half past seven. You order another coffee and a bottle of sparkling water. The receptionists are salacious and you exchange courtesies on route to the hotel entrance. Once outside Boland is grinning and you attempt to conceal any disappointment at seeing him again.

"Morning, Captain," he's holding out his hand, which you shake. He's wearing navy trousers, pale blue shirt and ultra-thin yellow tie. His suit jacket is absent in favour of a light green high visibility jacket, which has the company logo on the back.

"Did you sleep well, Captain?" he asks.

"A splendid night's rest Mr Boland. I like the colour of that jacket, is it green?" you reply sarcastically, which he ignores.

"This way please, sir," a large ruddy faced man in a black linen suit, and white shirt states. You and Boland follow him past the hotel for no more than five minutes. He stops at a gargantuan site and stares at Boland, awaiting further instructions.

It's an impressive building, which you could see being constructed from your apartment. There is the unmistakable logo hanging from the seven-storey block. However, instead of the colour green, the building is a plethora of dark blues, purples and pinks.

"This is something Sir Terence is very proud of. It's taken the best part of six months to fully construct and we're now in the final stages. They're adding electrics, décor and some furniture. Every unit is to be occupied by any new migrant that is willing to work," he says, beaming with pride.

"How do you know if they're willing to work?" you ask him, perplexed by the notion.

"They will all be employees in Sir Terence's various business operations. They will be cooks, cleaners, waiters and bar staff," he replies before continuing.

"A prerequisite for these capsule apartments is being on Sir Armstrong's payroll," he says before pausing for potential questions.

"How will waiters and bar staff afford such luxurious accommodation?" you enquire.

"The first three months accommodation is free. Only then will members of this community gradually begin to contribute to the living costs," he outlines.

"That is generous," you respond with feigned enthusiasm.

"It's an investment Captain. Sir Terence wants to provide the new comers to this great nation with incentives."

"Three months' rent is quite an inducement," you reply and grin back ruefully.

"Sir Armstrong believes in the great capacity of human beings. These individuals might start off as cleaners but after a few years their children will be the next marketing directors and doctors. Combined with our successful Education Foundation we're all optimistic for the future of our city," he says overzealously.

"What about the news this morning?" you interrupt him abruptly.

"What news?" he asks, looking vexed and confused why you've halted his flow.

"Sir Terence was commenting on recent migrants to the city. A young male student was beaten to near death a few nights ago. Sir Armstrong believes in strong leadership," you summarise the article you've just read. Boland looks furious and his top lip curls. The overly shaped right eyebrow rises inquisitively before his whole face changes into a broad smile.

"Exactly. That's what we're attempting here. If those young men had been employed and had more direction, such incidents would never happen," he pleads with you.

"It seems a rather mixed message, Mr Boland," you respond.

"Sir Terence is trying to alleviate the burden from the government. He's in an enviable position, financially speaking, to promote programs, building enterprises and job opportunities. This will create a society of grateful individuals who have been given a second chance the minute they arrive on these shores. You must have seen the torments these poor creatures go through in your time at border control?" he asks.

"And Sir Terence expects nothing in return for his efforts?" you ask politely.

"Self-interest is the last thing on his mind," he replies curtly.

Chapter 31

Damian Boland is attempting to remove dirt from his wicker loafers, which are peculiar footwear on a construction site.

"I was informed yesterday evening that this mess would be cleared, at least for the ground floor apartments," he explains, looking vexed.

"No problem," you reply, knowing that it's more of an issue for him and his delicate footwear.

"This way, Captain," he says despondently and you follow him the ground floor doors. The décor of the corridor is pleasant and the walls are covered with Japanese art.

"Sir Terence sees these apartments as an urban village, rather than the unsightly capsule flats that currently dominate our skyline," he says, ushering into the first apartment.

There are tastefully painted canvases of coastal seas but the flat is sparse and soulless. The kitchen is minute and opens in an area that deigns to be a lounge. He shows you the separate room, which contains a long showering room. The shower could hold up to six people, which you fear is the intention.

"This apartment can hold seven residents," he tells you with pride.

"Is that ideal?" you enquire.

"It means that families aren't torn apart. Many migrants can't physically inhabit the small spaces they've previously been housed in. These flats are compact but luxurious," he states before pulling down one of several beds from the walls.

"The bed only remains grounded when someone is sleeping on it. This makes it easier to fold back into the wall," he continues.

"Very luxurious," you reply sardonically and feel the rough exterior of the bed linen.

"We're hoping that after the success of this building, we can encourage government funded apartments based on similar designs," he expounds enthusiastically.

"How often does Sir Terence meet with the government agencies?" you ask.

"There are no scheduled meetings but Sir Terence has established successful relationships with leading members of His Majesty's Government," he explains.

"I hear Sir Armstrong is very close friends with His Majesty?" you respond.

"They were educated together; share the same beliefs, hopes and dreams for this great country. This is not a secret Captain and is common knowledge amongst the press. Neither the King nor Sir Terence has hidden their deep affection for one another," he states diplomatically and you smile back in recognition.

"Now if you'll follow me, I'll show you something quite extraordinary," he continues. Boland leads you out of the apartment and into the lift.

"When will the other apartments be finished?" you enquire.

"We have been assured that full completion of our urban village will be in three weeks yesterday," he replies professionally and then presses a light green button. There is the letter MF emblazoned on the front and you tilt your head squinting at Damian Boland.

"It stands for Meditation Floor," he explains proudly. The lift doors slide open and you enjoy the soft breeze air. He notices your relief before commenting.

"The air conditioning is to be connected tomorrow afternoon. Please let me show you the 'Meditation Floor'. The entire floor in pine flooring and includes a small circular pool in the centre. There are a dozen open-air booths with protection from the glare of the sun. Inside them are light green cushions, you assume to sit on when meditating. It's very minimalist with just a few artificial plants situated in key areas. You notice freshly installed speakers in the four corners of the floor."

"Do they work?" you ask inquisitively and point at two of the speakers.

"Fantastic. You'll love this," he claims rather presumptuously. There is a switch on the side of all the booths and he presses one firmly. There are different noises coming from the various speakers. The nearest one sounds like the sea crashing onto rocks, there is the distant music of an acoustic guitar and slow chimes echo across the pine floor.

"It's beautiful, don't you think, Captain," he closes his eyes and smiles broadly.

"Very pleasant," you reply looking at him with bewilderment.

"I'll take you back to the hotel now," he returns to his business like tone.

"Thanks," you respond politely and follow him back into the lift and out on to the street.

"There will be food served in the hotel lounge at twelve. They can bring this to the room if you so desire. At half one I'll take you to see Sir Terence for a follow up meeting," he outlines the plans for this afternoon and then shakes your hand before leaving.

When you walk into the hotel entrance you see the receptionist marching quickly to you. He's a diminutive middle-aged man, with a bald patch made more visible by his lack of height. In his left hand is a folded piece of paper.

"Captain, this message was left for you about ten minutes ago," he seems slightly flustered and is sweating profusely. You open the note and immediately recognise the handwriting. The message is from Matt Wraith and he wants to meet you in a nearby café. Apparently he has someone for you to speak with.

"I appreciate this," you say, holding up the paper like a binding legal document. He nods back and then rushes back to the reception, having noticed a small queue forming.

"I'll be dining out today," you say to the receptionist before you leave the hotel.

Café Quimperle is a five-minute walk from the hotel and Matt Wraith is sitting outside on a blue metal chair. He's sipping from a small espresso coffee and has lit one of his distinctive all white cigarettes. He's wearing loose fitting beige trousers with the hems rolled up. You've never seen him dressed so casually and smile at his white top with navy blue stripes. On his feet are distinctive tan deck shoes with no socks.

"Are you on holiday, Matt?" you ask wryly and he smiles back. Wraith then leans back in his chair to get the attention of a waiter.

"A black coffee please," he asks a young attractive red haired girl with pale skin.

"Decaf with pouring cream please," you add, when the girl approaches your table.

"Are you eating?" she asks and you both nod enthusiastically, whilst she places two menus on the table. Matt watches her intently as she walks over to place the order.

"Very nice," says Matt Wraith, raising his left eyebrow knowingly.

"Isn't she a little on the young side?" you state and grin back.

"Some of us are still young, old friend," he replies, grinning broadly.

"Who is this person you think I should meet?" you ask him, returning to more pressing matters.

"He was one of many assistants to Sir Terence. He's called Samuel Curley and will be here at midday. Does that give you enough time to get back?" Wraith asks you.

"More than enough time," you say watching the waitress bring the coffee.

"I don't suppose you mind if I have a glass of beer do you? I know it's still early days for you isn't it?" he asks you earnestly. When people have asked you this in previous dry spells this would have sent your mind racing.

"I don't mind at all," you reply and you mean it too.

Chapter 32

Matt Wraith takes a large gulp from his ice-cold beer and looks up into the sun. He pulls the sleeves of his Breton top up, relishing the glorious weather. Your friend then removes a packet of French tobacco from his trousers, taking out a slim white cigarette. In the opposite pocket Matt reveals a gold lighter, which he uses to deftly light his cigarette.

"This Curley is a nervous type," he states, exhaling the thick smoke from his mouth.

"Why did he leave Armstrong's employment?" you enquire.

"His contract was terminated about three months ago. Curley was caught with stimulants during working hours. This isn't irregular in itself, with thousands of the city's population using them for work. Unfortunately for him, he was found wandering round a staff meditation suite shouting incoherently. He'll be here in about five minutes," Wraith explains, and leaves his cigarette burning in the ashtray.

"I'll be back in a moment," he says, gesturing towards the men's room.

This leaves you panic-stricken and you stare hypnotically at the remnants of his beer on the table. You begin to feel cold sweat pouring from the forehead and anxiety rising through your left arm. The incessant thoughts are neutralised when you remember that's all they are, thoughts.

"Do you have a spare Euro?" says the disgruntled voice and you look up from the table. In front of you are three destitute looking young men, all no older than twenty-five. Their faces are smeared in dirt and one of them is clasping a small bottle of vodka. The one asking the question is surprising well dressed in a stainless white linen shirt and denim trousers. His two comrades are more jaded both wearing dark unkempt tracksuits.

"I'm afraid I don't have any," you reply and they move on to their next sales pitch. You feel great sympathy and some empathy for these poor souls. It's difficult to greet these groups with any consistency. Whether you give them money can depend on their politeness, your mood, their gender and age. The city is populated with hundreds of similar cases roaming the streets, and you know there is no immediate solution.

"That's him," states Matt Wraith over your shoulder. He takes his seat and points at a figure approaching the café. Sam Curley is about six foot tall and extremely thin. He's wearing khaki trousers and a white t-shirt, which hangs off his body. Curley nods at Matt in recognition and approaches your table. You both shake his sweat-ridden palm and try to ease his obvious discomfort.

"Drink?" Wraith asks him.

"Can I get a vodka?" he replies sheepishly.

"A large glass of vodka please and leave the bottle please," your friend bellows to the nearest waiter. You notice the anxiety dissipate from the man's face. This is a look and a feeling you know only too well. The overwhelming relief that alcohol has been procured is clear on his line-ravaged face. Matt pours from the vodka bottle into a thick-based glass and using both hands your guest gulps down the drink. He begins to wretch but manages to keep the alcohol in before leaning back into his chair.

"What information do you have, Mr Curley?" you ask directly, not wanting to prolong this cross-examination.

"Tell the Captain what you told me," urges Wraith.

"I was one of Sir Terence Armstrong's personal assistants. There are only ever four of these at any given time. I was privy to all confidential meetings, except when Sir Terence would discuss things with Mr Boland. This was always private," he explains, wiping sweat from his brow. Matt pours him another drink and he continues,

"Sir Terence has a very clear set of goals and he is ruthless in carrying them out," Curley says conspiratorially.

"What goals?" you demand impatiently.

"All the marketing campaigns and charity work is a façade. The new capsule hotels and media image cover up his real intentions. He wants the top job," he whispers.

"Does he want to be King?" you say sarcastically and smile at Matt. However, he doesn't grin back and admonishes you with a cold stare.

"I was in countless meetings when it was constantly referred to using deliberately ambiguous language, obviously." Sam Curley takes another sip of his drink.

"What top job does Armstrong want?" he asks. "Head of Government," he states plainly. This makes you laugh and nod your head from side to side in disbelief.

"Why on earth would one of the most powerful men on the planet secretly desire a thankless role like that?" you ask, still affronted at this waste of valuable time.

"I don't know but that is the whole purpose of everything they do at the Head Office. You should see the people he's met with; foreign ministers, corrupt businessmen and criminal elements." He continues,

"Criminal elements?" you ask quietly.

"Eastern European gangs, anti-government terrorists, youth gangs and even jaded academics. Do you know John Werther?" he asks passionately.

"Yes, we know him. What was John Werther doing there?" you exclaim.

"He was in and out of the Head Office every day and there was talk about him being employed as an Educational Consultant. But he couldn't stay away from his students could he? I had to set up meetings with impoverished young undergraduates for him. An appalling use of power, which makes me feel sick just thinking about what I did," he shudders.

"Tell him about Dudek," Matt Wraith interrupts.

"I only met him once, a friendly young man. He'd met with Sir Terence a couple of times under the diplomatic umbrella of migration policy. Then Dudek went off the radar and Sir Armstrong went ballistic. He very rarely lost his temper," he claims.

"What did he do?" you ask him gently, observing his face contorting in concentration.

"He threw a decanter of whiskey at Mr Boland and obliterated a pine chair in his office. He demanded to speak to his contacts in the various government departments. The man was absolutely livid," he looks pained recalling these memories.

"Did anyone from the government get in contact?" you ask him softly, determined not to startle him.

"There were several liaisons organised through Mr Boland. These meetings were always discreetly planned with only Sir Terence and Mr Boland invited. They were always very careful about that. When I saw Dudek had been killed I knew what had happened."

He looks at Matt for sympathy. Wraith has noticed you're now completely dumbfounded.

"Did you report this, Sam?" Matt Wraith asks your guest.

"No. I'd become petrified and couldn't look anyone at work in the eye. I'd always been a big drinker who used stimulants if I needed to meet a deadline. It helped me stay focused," he explains and you nod you head empathically.

"Very soon I was out of control. I'd drink first thing in the mornings just to stop the shaking and vomiting. When they found me in the bathroom at work I was a shambles. I hadn't eaten for two weeks."

"What did they do?" you ask him.

"They gave me a very generous leaving package. My pension intact and a clear signal that if I opened my mouth to anyone there would be severe consequences," he breathes out with relief.

"Why tell us now?" you say with genuine bewilderment.

"I can't sleep. I had to tell someone."

He stops talking as quickly as he began and looks down solemnly at the café floor.

"Thank you, Sam." You press your arm onto his shoulder.

Chapter 33

Matt Wraith is escorting the shambolic Mr Curley to the nearest tram stop, no doubt compensating him for his time and information on route. You have remained seated and stir a hot chocolate slowly, unable to fathom what you've heard. There is tightness in your stomach, which is more uncomfortable than the one your recovering body has acclimatised to. There isn't enough time to think rationally and hypothesise the people Armstrong spoke to in the government. The corruption doesn't surprise or anger you, but your inability to question these facts at the time leaves you feeling emasculated. It's ten past one and you rise from your chair and walk rapidly back to the hotel.

Outside the hotel is Boland, accompanied by two thickset men in black linen suits. You breathe slowly in and exhale through the nose. He has an inane grin plastered on his over moisturised face, with his highly manicured right hand held out. Boland smells horrifically of unisex cologne, which you thought no longer, existed.

"It's a shame you didn't dine at the hotel Captain. They were serving steak, spinach and chips. I sometimes go there myself when I know it's being served," he exclaims.

"I decided to get some fresh air," you reply.

"Yes. I see that," he states, looking disappointed you've deviated from his meticulous plans.

"We have a car waiting for us, Captain," he returns to his business like delivery.

"A car?" you enquire, casually observing his two associates. They both have their haircut close to the head and neatly trimmed at the back of the neck. One is about an inch taller than you and extremely toned with broad shoulders and keen hazel eyes. The other man is smaller but more muscular and his black suit looks painted on.

"Yes. Sir Terence thought it would be pleasant to continue your discussion outside of the Armstrong Family. There is a bar he's fond of, which is about a fifteen-minute drive from here," Boland replies, gesturing to the shorter man to fetch the vehicle. You can't remember the last time you travelled in a car. They became fashionable ten years ago, when leading manufacturers in the Far East began producing affordable electric vehicles in minimalist styles. You remember fondly how you and the kid, after several drinks with Mike Flannery, spent twenty minutes laughing at a city worker trying to charge his car at an 'energy spot'. The energy spots were just huge batteries, which either melted in the heat or became inoperable after only a few weeks. You recall reading about Sir Terence urging the government to re-invest in small environmentally friendly vehicles, like the ones you saw in France.

The car that Boland's assistant drives towards you is the most impressive you've seen. It lacks the loud humming noise that could irritate on the French models and can fit in five or six passengers. It's painting jet black and glistens in the sunlight.

"She's impressive isn't she?" asks Boland, as if referring to naval vessel.

"On the outskirts of the city, Sir Terence had her travelling up to a hundred miles per hour. This was under strict safety regulations," he continues.

"Of course," you reply sardonically and climb into one of the back seats. You lean back into the leather upholstery and watch with amusement as Damian Boland ambles in to the seat beside you.

"Please fasten your belts, gentlemen," asks the driver before pulling the vehicle out onto the main street. The car slowly follows the tramline through the city centre, rarely getting above twenty miles per hour. You stare outside the window, trying to conceal the embarrassment of being pointed at by commuters and small children.

"Here we are, gentlemen," announces the driver, just over ten minutes into the journey.

"I can't leave the car here, but you better get out now sir," the smaller of the robust men states.

"Thank you," replies Boland and opens the car door. You watch him descend onto the pavement, noticing how dust covered his wicker loafers have become. You are standing outside an exclusive restaurant and bar called 'Central'.

"Please follow me, Captain," Mr Boland asks, whilst watching the car drive away.

There are five immaculate black chrome tables set for dining. Only two of the outside tables are in use, with a group of four men in suits sitting at the first. They're adorned it expensive lightweight suits, in various shades and patterns of grey. All the men are in the late thirties, wearing white or pink shirts with the top two buttons undone and no tie. One of the men is dominating the conversation and keeps adjusting a hair band hanging over his slicked back hair. The others are all wearing dark shades, despite being seated in the shade and smoking earnestly. On the table are plates of untouched salads and four thick-based glasses of whiskey. The group leader raises his glass and barely sips the drink, which makes you grin.

The second table is occupied by two young women in their mid to late twenties. They are both extremely attractive and surrounded by shopping bags. The first young lady has bleached blonde hair with a cropped fringe, heavily shadowed eyes and made up face. She's breathing out smoke through her generous lips. Her dress is designed to look like a man's pale blue shirt with a five-inch belt holding the garment to her body. Her companion is a gorgeous brunette in white cut off trousers, wooden clogs and a low cut top revealing her cleavage. At the centre of their table is a large bottle of white wine in a bucket of ice water. You follow Boland past the two tables and smile at two females.

"Good afternoon, ladies," you say warmly and notice the brunette smile back, whilst the other looks annoyed that her conversation has been interrupted. Boland gives you a stark look and you smile back like a mischievous infant.

"I think the blonde one liked your shoes, Mr Boland," you state dryly and follow him inside into 'Central'. There is a small queue developing behind a studious looking man in a navy tuxedo, who seems to be directing people to tables. He acknowledges Boland and nods towards a table at the far end of the expansive room. Sitting on his own sipping a large measure of whiskey is Sir Terence Armstrong. As you approach the table with Boland and one of the black suited aides, he stands up revealing a beautifully tailored pale blue suit. It's been taken in above the waist that extenuates his slim but muscular build. He's wearing a crisp white shirt and peach coloured tie. On his feet are freshly polished tan loafers over socks that match his tie.

"Please take a seat, gentlemen," he says, shaking your hand firmly and offering you a seat.

"I thought we might continue our conversation in a more relaxed environment. Would you like a drink?" he asks you.

"Just a small glass of sparkling water please," you reply politely.

"Are you sure? I'm sure the government would allow you a minor indiscretion? This is my second scotch and I can testify that it definitely works. It's sixty years old," he says and then smiles broadly.

"No thank you, Sir Terence," you respond.

"We have a sensible man here Boland," he states to his assistant before catching the eye of a waiter. A middle-aged man wearing black trousers, burgundy braces over a white shirt and a small bow tie approaches the table.

"What can I get you, Sir Terence?" he asks dutifully.

"I'll have another one of these please Nigel. A glass of sparkling water and what would you like Boland?" Armstrong enquires.

"A large gin and tonic please, sir," says Damian Boland.

"Right away, sir," states the diligent waiter.

"And feel free to surprise us with some food please, Nigel," adds Sir Terence with finality.

Chapter 34

You take a large sip of the sparkling water and place the thick-based glass on the table. The aide is now relaxing at the bar with a glass of beer, his eyes roaming the room for any potential assailants. The waiter has left three plates of food in the centre of the table, after Armstrong's request. The plates are imposingly large but cuisine is sparse and decorated in various blends of sauce. The first plate has five thin slices of salmon graphitised by yellow sauce, with an inconspicuous slice of lemon. On the middle plate are a handful of fish pastries, again adorned in bright sauce. The final plate contains three small pieces of chicken covered in rice and peppers.

"Do you know how I feel after I've eaten here, Captain?" asks Sir Terence.

"Hungry?" you ask coldly. There is a small pause before Armstrong laughs heartily and points his finger at you in faux admonishment.

"The portions might be slight but the food here is exquisite. I paid for the chef to move here a year ago. He was running a coastal restaurant in Brittany. A beautiful place but only a handful of people would eat there. He had no concept of marketing and no business acumen," he replies.

You reach out to the middle plate and consume a pastry. It's a diplomatic gesture, which Sir Terence appreciates and he smiles warmly. He pulls back his chair and crosses his right leg over his left, with the ankle resting on the opposing knee. Sir Terence Armstrong then takes a large sip from his glass and stares at you intensely.

"I did know William Dudek," he states with a slow monotonous delivery. You can feel your heart begin to race and beat heavily against the chest. You'd like to run out of the restaurant away from here. There's probably a small bar nearby, where you could relieve this anxiety with two large glasses of anything. It wouldn't concern you whether it was vodka, whiskey or brandy and the label would be irrelevant. The mind racing would cease and the anxiety would dissipate within minutes. Unfortunately, this would eventually lead to cataclysmic disaster. The first bout of consumption might be moderate, but within days or weeks the inevitable would occur. The morning drinking would return and the incessant dry retching, relieved only by another bout would continue. You stay in your seat and sit with this pain.

"Are you okay, Captain?" Boland enquires sarcastically.

"Yes," you manage to reply, feeling the strain on a dry throat. Boland looks across at his superior and grins at his co-conspirator.

"The government knew that I wished to speak with all parties. It was important to talk to leading members of all the resistance groups. They didn't broadcast this in the papers but it was common knowledge within the higher echelons of the government ministries," Armstrong explains, leaning forward to extract maximum empathy. This is nonsense and your heart continues to beat rapidly. Unfortunately, you know the importance of feigning complete ignorance.

"And William Dudek was one of these leaders?" you ask calmly. Sir Terence slides his chair back under the table predatorily and consumes a slice of the salmon.

"Every precaution was taken Captain. I'm not reckless enough to meet an individual like Dudek without being accompanied. If I can understand what makes these people so enraged with our society, we can produce consensual solutions. We can all work together and produce a fair society, which we are all proud to be part of. In continually labelling these groups as terrorists or anarchists, we are further from finding out why they behave like this," he outlines, using his hands to emphasis his key points.

"I don't believe that anyone living in this city wants to systematically destroy the fabric of our society," he continues with a pained look on his face. The anxiety that swept through the arms has been slowly replaced with anger.

"What solutions do you suggest?" you ask him earnestly

"You've seen it today! The things that Boland has shown you," he exclaims enthusiastically.

"It's integral that we build up a sense of community in our young. That's why I encourage all the sporting activities and local community foundations. The apartments that you've seen today are the next step. Instead of the cramped infestations that breed criminal behaviour, we offer an alternative. The families stay together and live together in more spacious luxuriant homes," his tone is statesman like.

"Drinks," Boland says clearly. This has the desired effect of halting Sir Armstrong from his diatribe.

"Good idea," you reply in agreement. The waiter comes across and takes another round of drinks and you notice for the first time that Sir Terence appears drunk. He isn't slurring his words or falling from his chair but there is a glazed look developing on the eyes.

"What was your impression of Dudek?" you ask keenly, now aware that Armstrong may inadvertently reveal something compromising. Boland's smile desists and he stares at you disapprovingly.

"He was a very promising, intelligent young man. It's always tragic when such an individual dies before fulfilling their potential," he says, looking away from the table.

"What did you ask him?" you attempt to probe him further and Boland maintains his disapproving glare.

"We discussed many issues about the city. Reasons why migrants are vilified in the media, crimes in the capsule apartments and even environmental issues," he continues. This last part is the most obvious lie. The Kid had no enthusiasm for the environment and spent twenty minutes once tearing into Mike Flannery. Mike had installed a recycling machine at the back of his bar, after a government advertising campaign aimed at small businesses. Dudek found this hilarious and completely pointless, considering the other problems in the city.

"I refuse to ignore the more salubrious parts of the city and I'm keen to meet the more colourful members of the community too. If only the government felt the same way, Captain," he replies.

"I thought you worked in tandem with the government, Sir Terence?" you ask him dryly.

"My colleagues and friends in the government can only achieve so much though," he responds in an aggressive way. Boland leaps to his feet and places his arm on your shoulder.

"I think it's time we returned you to the hotel, Captain," Boland says in his officious manner and nods at the aide, who walks over from the bar.

"I do have a couple of more questions," you say sardonically.

"I'm afraid my assistant Mr Boland is quite right Captain. I've had a very busy schedule this morning. It's important for me to relax, but perhaps this many scotches so early in the day aren't advisable," he says, caressing his glass of scotch and looking at the contents inquisitively.

"I may have been over keen to explain my plans," he says with finality.

"You've been very candid," you reply grinning back triumphantly.

"Please, Captain," interrupts Boland and you shake hands with Sir Terence Armstrong firmly.

"Thank you for a short but illuminating chat," you say politely and then let Boland escort you out of the restaurant.

"Did you meet William Dudek?" you ask Boland, once the three of you are back outside. He doesn't reply to your question and guides you politely back into the car. Sir Terence Armstrong has argued succinctly that he would like to create a city community, based on consensus. You don't know what he really desires, but it isn't this.

Chapter 35

It's twenty past five in the morning when you wake up, and the light is shining through the inadequate blinds. They are based on the latest trend from the Far East. The white paper blinds are painted with red Japanese engravings and stuck to the wall with adhesive. When you woke, as you do frequently at the moment the stark red symbols startled you. It was nearly three in the morning before you slipped back into slumber. This presents no problems and you still get just over six hours rest. In recovery you've felt invigorated and optimistic in the mornings, thriving on little sleep. You relish feeling fresh in the morning and shower quickly and change.

Poe made certain that more of your things would be sent to the hotel if your stay were to be extended. When you returned late yesterday evening, a concierge informed you that a government officer had delivered some items. Two suits, three shirts, four ties some documents on Boland's known background and some casual clothes you'd packed previously. After putting on a slim fit navy suit, pale blue shirt and a woollen tie identical in colour to the suit, you scan through Boland's file with an espresso in the hotel café.

There is nothing spectacular about Boland's previous employment or education. He achieved below average grades from an elite private school before achieving a high standard degree at a mediocre University. He's spent several years working in marketing throughout the city before gaining dutiful employment with Sir Terence Armstrong. You can imagine him ingratiating himself with his superiors in what, on paper looks like a meteoric rise. At the back of this information is a confirmation memorandum. The administrators at Poe's office have confirmed that the two black suited aides were spotted at Dudek's meetings with Armstrong. After eating two croissants and some honey and porridge you set off for your meeting with Colonel Poe.

Outside you are greeted with the surreal sight of a young girl performing gymnastics. The two trams travelling in opposing directions have stopped in front of the large spherical red lights. She back flipped onto the crossroad as you stepped out on to the streets, smiled and waved at early commuters on the trams before performing a handstand. She's wearing cycling shorts beneath her dishevelled dress and you notice a nearby couple applauding. Just before the lights turn green she retains her normal posture and takes a bow. The incident has clearly thrilled onlookers in and around the trams. You smile as the petite brunette girl walks past and continue walking.

It's nearly eight when you notice Colonel Poe sat outside Café Scoff. Poe is dressed as indiscreetly as you've seen him. He's wearing large beige shorts, pink polo shirt, leather sandals and large circular sunglasses.

"Good morning, sir," you say pleasantly.

"Good morning, Captain!" he says jovially and orders to espressos.

"Would you like some food?" he enquires.

"Perhaps we could have ice cream," you reply inspecting his outfit. He immediately notices the inference, starts laughing and tugs on his polo shirt.

"My wife has insisted that I wear more casual clothes. We aren't meeting to discuss men's fashion though. How is the investigation proceeding?" he asks in the formal way you've become accustomed to.

"Sir Armstrong has admitted the kid was an acquaintance. He makes no qualms over the people he liaises with, criminals, migrants and government employees," you state.

"Has he named anyone in the government specifically?" asks Poe.

"He's too smart for that, even after several midday cocktails. I'm almost certain he knows who I am too," you respond tentatively.

"What do you mean?" Poe asks politely before sipping from his recently arrived espresso.

"The way he behaved yesterday, knocking back expensive spirits so early in the day. It was like he was goading me sir," you explain.

"I trust he was unsuccessful?" he enquires.

"Yes but I'm convinced that he knows that I eliminated William Dudek," you say coldly.

"How would he know who you are?" Poe asks you and stirs the remains of his coffee.

"How could he not know? Armstrong has informants and colleagues embedded in every government apartment."

"What do you surmise our Knight of the Realm is up to then?" Poe asks sarcastically.

"I believe that he is seeking the very highest office sir. He views himself as a saviour of the city. Its protector." you say and then sip from your espresso.

"That would be unprecedented Captain, lay persons don't get to become leaders, however corrupt the system and no matter how rich the individual," outlines Colonel Poe.

"What if there was a crisis?" you ask your superior.

"What type of crisis?" he asks and smiles ruefully.

"It could be one of many. A terrorist attack, a high profile killing or a government official killed. I don't know exactly but Sir Armstrong isn't the raconteur, family man and environmentalist the media portrays," you continue.

"You could be right, Captain," Poe replies cautiously and then continues.

"This is a very delicate matter Captain. Sir Armstrong has done a great deal of charitable work for the city and his building plans are very popular with several government departments. Not to mention his close relationship with His Majesty." Poe describes the situation calmly.

"But proceed with the investigation," you ask.

"Yes," he responds emphatically and moves his polo shirt about, creating a makeshift fan.

"However, try to find out what he's planning," the Colonel continues.

"And then?" you ask, seeking more clarity.

"Ruffle feathers Captain. I did not assign you this task because of your finesse or for an abundance of tact. Just be sure that when you do act upon your judgement, that there is proof," he explains diplomatically.

"Thank you, sir," you respond back dutifully in the knowledge that you have the Colonel's full backing. There are very few people that you trust however, Colonel Poe is one of them.

"I trust you can take care of the bill. We are paying you enough these days and you can't squander all of your wages on new shoes," he smiles and then stands up from his seat.

"No problem, Colonel," you reply and pick up the bill left by the adolescent waiter.

"How is your other matter?" he asks and places his right palm on your left shoulder.

"I'm good, sir. The mind still races but I'm picking up tools every day," you reply.

"Excellent. Well Captain, don't hang around here all day staring at women. You have an assignment to complete," he says warmly and then sets off towards the nearby tram stop.

Boland arranged with you yesterday afternoon to make your own way to Armstrong's Head Office for ten o'clock. He'd like to take you to the factory floor, where Armstrong products are assembled. This leaves you time to buy another coffee, walk the streets, read the newspaper and smoke a couple of the thin cigars from the silver plated holder in your jacket pocket. You feel more confident in the assignment, with Colonel Poe's explicit backing.

"Can I have another coffee please?" you ask the young waiter, as he collects the crisp ten Euro note you've left.

Chapter 36

You leave a meeting two hours after the discussion with Poe. When you normally vacate a meeting a blanket of serenity accompanies it. Unfortunately, today's gathering was sabotaged by one individual's ego. All identities remain anonymous but you know the type. She bulldozes everyone else's opinions, using rudeness masked as honesty. A trait that you know is familiar with people from the area in the North, she was undoubtedly from. You still feel pacified and grateful that your own recovery is based on quality rather than quantity. They boasted of their decades of what sounded like tortuous sobriety. This is something that you promised yourself you would avoid at all costs.

It's a rare grey day, with small flecks of rain trickling down your shaved head. The heat is still intense and you notice a large man in his forties outside the hotel with an expansive sweat stain on his back. Boland is waiting directly behind him, with an impatient look on his face. He's wearing an exceptional well-cut navy linen suit, ruined by appalling cheap tan loafers that point up around the toes like a circus clown.

"You're ten minutes late, Captain," he exclaims, gesturing to his watch.

"I thought I was being given free rein today? To investigate the main building by myself," you reply irritably.

"I still need to issue you with the relevant passes and get you to sign the relevant papers. This was all highlighted in our original correspondence with the Government departments," he continues.

"I do apologise, Mr Boland," you reply diplomatically and grasp the digital card from his left hand. It allows access to all the various floors of the Armstrong Head Office.

"That's quite all-right Captain. Please sign this document and we will send your department a copy before the end of today," he removes a double-sided piece of paper with the date already inscribed.

"I'm going to my room. No doubt I'll see you shortly," you state as you sign the paper dutifully.

You collect a small package from the hotel reception and then pace calmly to your room. The cleaner is just leaving the room and you smile politely.

"Hello, your room is ready," she says, with an indistinguishable eastern European accent. You nod back and enter the room. The freshly pressed linen and polished desk have left the suite feeling antiseptic. Its ice cold and you welcome the high quality air conditioning humming above the bathroom door. On the desk you unravel the tightly wrapped paper on the package. Inside is a government issued gun. They are all the same, a mated black colour about six inches long in a tan leather holster. You remove the gun from this and slide the gun into the back of your navy trousers. Then, as if preparing for battle you pull up your socks and bush a speck of dirt off the black tassel loafers.

When you arrive at the Armstrong Head Office, you are ushered through by security, who take a studied glace at your identity card. You decide to investigate the one area of the building that appeared prohibited. There is a young man in his early twenties stood officiously next to a door, and you approach him confidently.

"Excuse me, young man. What is on the lower ground floor?" you enquire cautiously. He's well over six feet tall and has broad shoulders, which bulge out of his grey suit.

"It's mainly a storage area, Captain," he responds quickly.

"You know who I am?" you ask and raise both eyebrows in mock surprise.

"Yes, sir," he says.

"I'd like to investigate that floor. Do I require an escort?" you state with more confidence.

"No, that isn't necessary. We've all been informed who you are and why you are here sir," he replies and then opens the door, pointing to the stairs that lead down.

"Thanks," you say genially and then stroll to a light green door that's ajar. You begin the brief ascent down the stairs and notice several lights flicker into life. The lower ground floor has the appearance of a recently completed and as yet unfurnished apartment. There are storage boxes leaning against the walls and a large desk at the far end of the floor. You hear footsteps behind you on the stairs, but your eyes remain fixed on the desk, with various documents and folders piled on top.

"Captain. Can we help you with anything?" the voice is warm and generous.

"I'm fine," you reply and don't turn round. You then feel a heavy blow between your neck and right shoulder blade. The eyes begin to glaze over and you feel the body struggle to remain upright. One knee follows another to the floor and you collapse feeling your head implode onto the ground. You then enter a dreamless sleep.

When you open your eyes, you're strapped to an uncomfortable chair. The back of your head is pounding in agony and your right shoulder blade is throbbing. On the floor is your tie and navy jacket. Above this is Damian Boland, who is grinning sadistically and glaring straight into your eyes. On his left, you notice his black suited, ruddy-faced chaperone. Sat on the opposite side and seated in another chair, is Sir Terence Armstrong.

"What's going on?" you ask. Boland looks at the large man with the gigantic bicep muscles bulging from his suit, and nods. The ruddy-faced man then calmly and efficiently thumps you in the right side of you face. The pain is instantaneous and you wince but don't yell out.

"That's quite a punch you have. Do you work out?" you say sarcastically and he then repeats the punch onto the left side of your face. The chair falls back and you're left horizontal on the floor, but still sat in the chair. Looking up at the beige ceiling, you smile ruefully.

"Are you still there?" you ask and feel blood drip down your face.

"Sit him up," Boland says coldly and your assailant props you back up. You tighten the abdominal muscles, half expecting another attack, but it doesn't arrive.

Sir Terence Armstrong is sat with his legs crossed, scratching the back of his neck. He's wearing a charcoal nail head fabric suit, with a sky blue shirt and no tie. The lighting is reflecting off the tip of his highly polished tan loafers.

"I would like to understand what you know. I'm fairly sure you know very little, unfortunately I can't afford to take the risk. You're not going to pretend this all comes as a surprise I hope?" he explains.

"No," you reply solemnly and wait for him to continue.

"Good. That will save a great deal of time and explanation. Mr Boland here doesn't like you and had all sorts of suggestions about how to make you more flexible. One idea was to force drink down you, getting you hideously drunk. Then throwing you back out there, in the hope you'd self-destruct," he says noticing the shock and exasperation in your face.

"Oh yes, Captain. We know all about you. The problem with Mr Boland's scheme was this ignored your stubborn nature. I knew you'd come back from that, just through sheer obtuseness. You were proving very helpful to our long-term plans," he smiles at the tortuous pained expression on your face.

"You have no idea what I'm talking about do you?" he asks without seeking a reply. He then arches his back and stretches.

"Why did you choose today to come to my humble abode with this?" he asks and then clicks his fingers at Boland. Damian Boland then walks forward holding out the government issued gun in his left hand.

Chapter 37

You glare at the gun resting in Boland's small effeminate hands and notice his well-groomed nails. Damian Boland's head is wobbling with rage and his eyes are squinting.

"Well?" he demands as a small bead of sweat falls of his sharply pointed nose. Boland the gun aloft and then swings it down onto the back of your head. The pain is instantaneous but you refuse to express this verbally. Sir Terence looks bewildered and signals at the black suited man to deal with an emotional Boland.

"Hasn't he got anything better to do? Isn't there some paper that needs folding?" you say through gritted teeth, dealing with the pain. This is what you have to do every day now, deal with the pain. You desist from hiding from the inevitable problems life presents. No more avoiding difficult thoughts and decisions. No more drinking.

"Please answer Mr Boland's question, Captain," says Armstrong in a clear measured voice.

"It's a very dangerous world and you can't be too careful," you reply dryly. Sir Terence stands up and slides his seat closer, before reseating himself.

"I suspect an explanation is probably overdue," states Armstrong sympathetically.

"This city and indeed this country is in crisis Captain. When I was a young man there was only one homeless man, and he wasn't homeless. After hours on the streets, he would pick up some shopping and get the tram home. I remember he'd be on the same tram, with my friends and I coming home from school," he outlines.

"I thought you went to a private school, Sir Terence," you ask pertinently but he ignores you and continues.

"This city is now swarmed with people begging for change, scouring bins for the remnants of cigarettes. There are to more migrants than ever. It seems to take nearly five minutes to order coffee because the waitress can't speak English," he pleads.

"Do you go out for coffee a lot?" you enquire sarcastically but again he ignores this.

"These migrants steal, pillage and petrify the citizens of this city. The government can't do a thing. Procedures, bureaucracy, budgets and fear bind them. The city and the country need an individual who isn't afraid to restructure the city," he says and grins broadly at you.

"Have you got anyone in mind?" you ask and he laughs uproariously, squeezing your left thigh.

"After a great deal on contemplation and reflection, I realised the situation had to deteriorate before it could improve. I would assist in this deterioration in various ways. I built more capsule apartments not less. Eighteen months ago I met the leader of a small but coercive group of polish migrants. At the time they were dismantling minute government placards and setting fire to departmental propaganda. I agreed to fund them, which allowed them to make more large scale assaults, like destroying buildings," he explains with relish, smiling at the recognition on your battered face.

"This individual became unpredictable and I decided it was important to have them neutralised. They could be another example of a city out of control. The masses would demand change from an emasculated government. They would demand fundamental change and look to a well-established saviour. I would naturally and humbly accept this challenge," he describes before a long sigh.

"That's all you wanted? To be in charge?" you ask, completely exasperated.

"Unfortunately, this young leader wasn't easy to find. The government agents we sent to apprehend him all failed. That's when your name was suggested to me Captain. You were perfect for this role, a high functioning alcoholic with links to the kid and everything to lose. We had hoped that after the assignment you'd go abroad and drink yourself to death. Unfortunately, you have a few friends in the government," he explains and you try to avoid eye contact, looking round the floor vacantly.

"What would you do differently to the government?" you ask desperately.

"They would go," he states coldly.

"Who?" you ask perplexed by his response.

"The migrant population would be relocated back to their homeland. The statutes have already been drawn up, there are several government ministers waiting for our first move," he states with a conspiratorial air.

"What about all the environmental campaigning you've done?" you ask.

"That's our way into the affections of the people. It's an issue they care about deeply, therefore it's an issue I must be seen to care about," he responds rapidly.

"This is all for power? You just want to be in charge?" you ask, aghast at the simplicity of Sir Terence's motivation.

"Yes," he states calmly and you smile, nodding your swelling head from side to side.

"Who sent you, Captain?" Armstrong asks politely. You shuffle in your chair and look in the opposite direction. This is intended to signify a total lack of cooperation and all three men sense this immediately.

"Most members of the government have become invaluable allies, however there are still a few rogue elements. I repeat my original question, who sent you?" he asks with more menace than previously.

"I was invited here by you, Sir Terence," you mumble and feel blood trickle down the back of your head. You feel disorientated and on verge of passing out. The breathing is becoming more laboured. Sir Armstrong gestures to a now passive Boland. Boland takes a bottle of water from the desk and pours some slowly into your mouth. You manage to consume most of it, despite some heavy coughing and he then pours more over the head.

"Don't fall asleep yet, Captain," he whispers in your ear. Your mind begins to race, at first you ponder whether they've just poured alcohol down your neck, but you're positive this hasn't happened. The thoughts then begin to find balance equilibrium, and you focus on positive themes. The evidence is now crystallised, the kid's assassination, the government leaks and the motives behind Armstrong's exploitation of the media.

If you can get to Poe and tell him what has been happening, you can check surveillance. There will be countless recordings and documents describing seemingly innocuous meetings between Armstrong and government ministers. These could be used and the whole scheme could be ripped apart.

"It seems that the Captain is refusing to cooperate Mr Boland," he smiles at his assistant knowingly.

"As I suspected, sir," he states with gratification.

"Very well, Boland, proceed but don't kill him yet," Armstrong says with finality and then leaves hastily up the stairs.

"I did ask you politely, Captain. Goodbye," Armstrong's voice echoes across the vast floor.

Boland looks at his dark suited ally, and then slides his right hand across his stomach. The ruddy-faced man stands over you menacingly and there are sweat beads cascading over his pockmarked face. His huge right arm swings back in an arch and his fist buries into your abdomen. He then repeats this movement with his left fist. These tasks are performed clinically and professionally, devoid of any subjective malice. You finally cry out in agony, before being sick.

"Who sent you, Captain?" asks Boland adjusting the strap on his watch.

"Piss off," you reply indignantly. If you could just get out of here and find Poe. The eyelids close over and sleep descends.

"Wake him up," commands Damian Boland.

Chapter 38

Your eyes are open but the head leans forward and you stare at the fresh blood on the floor. The last assault on your stomach knocked the seat onto the ground. The rope attaching to the floor became looser. For a few moments there was a glimpse of an opportunity. This disappeared once you were positioned upright during the blackout.

"You were my idea," claims Boland.

"What?" you ask, trying to sit up.

"I heard how you'd evaded incarceration, by working for the government. After reading your file, which was most entertaining, I suggested that it would be you who would kill Dudek," he explains with gleeful abandon. You need to goad him into striking you down again, or least enough for him to signal to the other man.

"I'm not going to tell you who sent me. We'll be here for a long time," you say, which has the desired effect.

He swipes at you with his left hand, which crashes across your left jaw. You know it would be reckless to wait for the other man to attack and you manipulate the momentum of Boland's feeble blow.

The front leg of the chair cracks in two and with relief you feel your body descend. You relax the muscles in an attempt to cushion the impact. The rope feels slacker around your back and chest. After rolling over, the chair leg falls off and it's possible to free your body and stand aloft. Boland is gripping the gun tentatively and his associate is striding towards you. You grab the unattached wooden leg and swing at the man's head before he strikes out. This measured movement knocks the large man unconscious and you move laboriously sideways, to view Boland. He's pointing the gun directly at you and his face has turned pale grey.

"Who sent you?" asks Damian Boland, but any confidence in his voice has evaporated. He looks displaced and petrified.

"Put my gun down on the floor," you instruct and notice how the adrenalin in your body is acting as a palliative to the pain. You walk at a slow pace till you are less than twenty centimetres from the tip of the weapon. You instinctively grab Boland's wrist and wrestle the piece from his hand. The gun falls to the ground and you pick it up, as quickly as your damaged body allows.

"Please, Captain," he says and then begins to whimper and let out a long seething hiss through his nose.

"How upstairs know what's happening here?" you ask him coldly, directing the gun at his chest.

"Only members of the security team," he claims and then fixes his glare on the gun.

"Stand over there," you gesture to the nearest wall.

"Why?" he whispers his enquiry and follows your instructions.

"Turn round!" you yell and watch him perform this task sheepishly. Before he can begin speaking again, you use the back of the gun as it baton. You hear the connection of the metal on the flesh around his skull and watch him collapse.

You consider trying to clean yourself up before fleeing the building, but opt to empty the pockets of your jacket. It's on the desk next to another water bottle, which you take a generous sip from. It would heroic to climb up the stairs, find Sir Armstrong and apprehend him. After this feat, you could fend off any security guards and find a way to Colonel Poe's government office. Then sit back and enjoy a victory parade and the accompanying plaudits. Unfortunately, in a few minutes the pain will become more acute and you'll barely be able to walk. Sir Armstrong will eliminate you and use the media to vilify your existence.

The gradient of the steps feel vast and it's a struggle to get to the ground floor. There are about four people wandering round reception and the daily running of a building now appears surreal. The exit is visible beyond the receptionists' area and there are two security guards stood imposingly by the door. The hope that you can make it to the two black suited men unnoticed becomes impossible. A young woman in her early twenties, wearing a red dress and beige heels starts screaming at you. For a moment you survey the terrain and observe the trail of blood you've left on the light green carpet. Both guards run from their posting near the door.

"Stand back, gentlemen!" you shout, but know this is a futile request. You pull back the trigger of the gun and aim at the larger of the two men's thigh. The blast from the government issued gun is loud and followed by a low bellow from the injured man. The other man becomes more cautious and takes slow steps back. When you leave the building he will follow you, apprehend you and possible knock you unconscious. You don't know the man's motives, how he came to work for Sir Terence and you don't care. You take aim and shoot him in his right foot. There is a middle-aged man walking through the door, and you shove them aside.

On the street you stagger towards the nearest tram stop, persistently looking back for anyone in pursuit. Fortunately there is only one other person at the tram stop, and a tram pulling in. A member of the cities destitute and ravaged has a half-finished bottle of vodka hanging out of his over-sized jacket. He takes a large gulp from the bottle, which makes you feel nauseous. In the distance there are three men running in your direction. The swelling hampers the vision in your right eye but one of the men would appear to be Sir Terence.

You slide onto the tram seat and rest your bloodied head against the glass. When the door closes, you see Sir Terence Armstrong outside, desperately trying to get one of the men with him to open the tram doors. You watch the expressions in his face with bewilderment. He looks on you menacingly, then with anger and then becomes more anxious. Finally, as the tram sets off you notice the look of astonishment on his face. It's like he can't imagine that someone would have the audacity to disrupt him from getting what he wants. It is the look of a frustrated stage director; appalled that one of his actors has deviated from the script.

The body is now enveloped in agony; the back, head and stomach sway in pain. There are body parts that felt fine, that now feel wretched. Your hands, which were able to grip the gun can't clench. Several fingers are broken and the prospect of getting out of the cheaply made yellow tram seats fills you with dread.

"Been in the wars, fella?" asks the vagrant who got on at your stop. He's holding out the vodka for you to take.

"No thanks pal. I'm good," you reply in a friendly tone.

"You don't look it, mate!" he slurs back and then laughs out aloud. He has no malice or anger in his manner and you smile back and nod in agreement.

In order to avoid passing out, through exhaustion and aching bones, you stand upright and grip an adjacent chair. Clinging to self-preservation you walk from the stop closest to the main Government offices. Within twelve minutes you're at the main reception, where one of the secretaries recognises you immediately.

"Captain. What's happened?" she gasps.

"I need to see Colonel Poe right now," you explain and then look over at the government Sergeant by the door.

"Secure the whole building sergeant. Make sure no one leaves," you shout as clearly as you can manage.

"Yes, sir," he replies dutifully.

It takes every effort at your disposal to make it to Poe's office with a young Corporal's assistance. Colonel Poe opens his office door and scans your appearance from head to toe. He's wearing a double-breasted charcoal grey pinstripe suit.

"What did you find out, Captain?" he asks excitedly.

"I found out everything, sir. The first thing we'll require is all surveillance records involving Armstrong. Could I get a hot chocolate too, sir?" you say in relief.

Chapter 39

It is a week later and you're lying in bed, taking measured sips on a piping hot Italian coffee. Matt Wraith brought it through four days ago, but you have waited for the wounds to heal before enjoying a cup. The nurse brought it to your room five minutes ago and you're enjoying observing the steam rising from the blend. You grasp a handful of ice-cold chocolates from a packet next to the bed. They taste exquisite and melt with the coffee and you lean back on to the upright pillow. The window is open and you close the eyes, listening to leaves being swept along the road outside. The hospital door opens abruptly, revealing Colonel Poe.

"The nurse told me you'd finally started drinking that French mud," he says disapprovingly.

"It's Italian, sir," you reply and grin broadly. He's wearing a three-piece chocolate brown suit, beige shirt and dark brown striped tie. His well-polished Chelsea boots add about an inch to his height.

"I've brought you a present!" he exclaims, holding a newspaper aloft.

"My supplies of chocolate could do with being replenished," you state dryly.

"I'll tell Sergeant Wraith to bring some over this evening," he states in a deadpan tone.

"The news is good," he says, turning round the newspaper to reveal the front page. There is a large image of Sir Terence Armstrong leaving a government interrogation centre. His face looks haunted and he's holding his arms hand at the side.

"We've not finished questioning him yet, but I've got what I need from Armstrong," Poe claims confidently.

"I assume incarceration is out of the question sir?" you ask.

"We can't afford the inevitable backlash. This is a very delicate situation," he replies and pours himself a drink from the coffee pot.

"My goodness this is excellent," he says, somewhat startled by the quality of the hot beverage.

"And Boland?" you enquire.

"Prison," he says quietly and takes another sip from the white china mug.

"Just Boland?" you ask.

"No, there are several arrests scheduled for tomorrow morning," he says before scanning the back pages of the newspaper.

"Who sir?" you say, before adjusting yourself and feeling a sharp pain in one of the broken ribs.

"Boland, several members of Armstrong's inner circle and five government Ministers, including the Minister of Trade."

"Garth Davies," you say the Ministers name clearly.

"Yes. He was receiving regular payments from Sir Terence and had drawn up the legal documents for proposed statutes. All sorts of ambiguous titles, one was called the Islands Liberation Act," he takes a deep breath, and then continues.

"The surveillance records showed us who we needed to investigate. It was then all about applying the right kind of pressure. There is a separate investigation underway on the housing contracts that Armstrong made with leading businesses," he explains.

"What happens to Armstrong?" you plead.

"He's finished. You've ruined his reputation and he will be forced into obscurity before the age of forty. Sir Terence Armstrong was never going to prison. This is a man who counted the King as a friend and despite his abhorrent activities has raised millions of Euros for charities," he raises his eyebrows in empathy.

"He killed people!" you bellow and then wince at the pain that this causes.

"So have we Captain," he replies solemnly and moves closer to the edge of the hospital bed.

"We are all culpable for something. Try to avoid using a moral compass in matters or you will become resentful and embittered. The world is rarely what we want it to be. If you can accept this, you will get more from life," he explains and you smile back in recognition.

"I'm missing my daily meditation, sir," you say playfully.

"You'll be out of here in three days; I'd like you to join me in my final interviews. Boland might be more vociferous in admitting his guilt, if you are in the room. It seems you gave him quite a shock," Poe tightens his tie.

"He was easily frightened, sir," you say in a light tone and Colonel Poe chuckles.

"After that I have a couple of reassuringly moribund assignments. I'd like you to return to the immigration port in France. Only a few days which will serve therapeutically. It's good to revisit the scene of a crime, when one is in a better frame of mind," he squints at you, looking for your acquiescence and you oblige him with a nod.

"What will my role be after this assignment?" you ask inquisitively.

"I'm sending you to Milan," he commands.

"Italy?" you ask.

"Yes. I thought your geography would cope," he replies sarcastically and then elaborates.

"I've decided to reinstate your previous rank in line with the pay increase we discussed yesterday. One of our ministers is attending a conference in Milan over a three day period," he states.

"When will I go?" you ask in anticipation.

"You will travel by train from Paris, arriving a week before the conference starts. It will be a straightforward surveillance operation; so don't feel obliged to work around the clock," he says warmly.

"Milan is a wonderful city and has remained more or less the same since climate change. It's incredibly hot, so you'll be relieved to know the hotel you're booked in has a pool," he smiles broadly and fills up you mug of coffee to the brim.

"Thank you, sir," you say with genuine gratitude.

"Any questions, Major?" he asks and straightens his back.

"None, sir," you reply officiously.

"Well, I shall leave you alone to read the paper in peace. Look after yourself and try not to worry about anything. You've done a fantastic job, now rest," he then leaves the room whistling down the outside corridor. The door soon re-opens with minutes and a nurse is stood over your bed.

"It's time for your swim, Captain," she says in a soft soothing way.

"Very well," you shuffle upright and avoid telling the young nurse that you're now a Major. Medical training probably doesn't incorporate military and governmental ranks.

She helps you slide into the lightweight wheelchair from the bed. In the changing rooms, you step into your sky blue swimming shorts. They feel loose around the waist, a key indicator of weight loss. This is unsurprising considering the recent stresses and spare portions of food offered in hospitals.

Once changed you observe your body in the vertical mirror. The old scars are now accompanied by new injuries. The bruising around the abdomen has changed colour and began to fade. You feel the injuries on the back of the shaved head but they're still sore. Outside the nurse is waiting by the pool and you shower yourself vigorously.

"It's lovely and warm, Captain," she says reassuringly, with her hand.

You step in and let yourself float on one of the long luminous tubes. It feels good to stretch out the muscles and swim one length of breaststroke. You then submerge yourself in the water before coming up to breathe near the steps.

"I think I'll have a few minutes in the steam room," you inform the nurse and enter the nearest room. You lay out on the wooden panels, breathing through your nose slowly. Colonel Poe was right, the World is rarely how we want it and you smile contently.

The End